Florence Warden

Ralph Ryder of Brent

Vol. II

Florence Warden

Ralph Ryder of Brent
Vol. II

ISBN/EAN: 9783337047986

Printed in Europe, USA, Canada, Australia, Japan

Cover: Foto ©Andreas Hilbeck / pixelio.de

More available books at **www.hansebooks.com**

\

RALPH RYDER OF BRENT

RALPH RYDER OF BRENT

A Novel

BY

FLORENCE WARDEN

AUTHOR OF

'THE HOUSE ON THE MARSH,' 'THOSE WESTERTON GIRLS,' ETC.

IN THREE VOLUMES

VOL. II.

LONDON

RICHARD BENTLEY AND SON

𝔓𝔲𝔟𝔩𝔦𝔰𝔥𝔢𝔯𝔰 𝔦𝔫 𝔒𝔯𝔡𝔦𝔫𝔞𝔯𝔶 𝔱𝔬 𝔥𝔢𝔯 𝔐𝔞𝔧𝔢𝔰𝔱𝔶 𝔱𝔥𝔢 𝔔𝔲𝔢𝔢𝔫

1892

RALPH RYDER OF BRENT

CHAPTER I.

THE entrance of the doctor, who came into the room just as old Mrs. Ryder was uttering her passionate warning, was a welcome relief both to Nanny and to her mother-in-law. The young wife knew that she would get from the elder lady no satisfactory answer to any of her questions; the latter was most anxious to escape from the ordeal of facing those searching eyes.

It seemed to Nanny, whose head
ached, and who was altogether in a
querulous, excited state, that the doctor
and her mother-in-law made common
cause in treating her as if she were too
young and frivolous a person to be of
much account in the house. The doctor
would not hear of her sitting up with
her husband, and said, ' You could do no
good, and only wear yourself out,' in a
tone which hurt her, making her feel
useless and in the way. Mrs. Bambridge
wanted to take her home with her, and
old Mrs. Ryder seconded the suggestion
with vigour. But Nanny insisted on
remaining at The Grange. She did not
feel satisfied that the intruder of the
afternoon had really left the premises.
There were plenty of nooks and corners
both in the house and about the grounds,

where a person familiar with the place might remain hidden for hours. Nanny knew that she should never feel safe again until she had met this person face to face, had found out whether it was or was not Lady Ellen, and what the real position of the lady was.

Until very late that night the unhappy young wife wandered, restless and lonely, about the house, listening at the door of the unused rooms, keeping watch in the long half-lighted corridors, on the alert at every sound. Old Mrs. Ryder and the nurse had finally turned her out of the sick-room, and told her to go to bed. Mrs. Bambridge had gone home, leaving one of her servants, who was to sleep on the ground-floor, so as to be within call of the nurse. A bedroom on the floor above had been hastily prepared for Nanny, who retired to it reluctantly, childishly frightened by the old-fashioned full-tester bedstead. So much, indeed, did it heighten the feelings of uneasiness and fear which had haunted the poor child all the evening, that she got upon the bed and tried to pull the curtains down. But they were so securely fixed that she had to give up the attempt, afraid of bringing down the whole rickety wooden erection upon her head.

Well, then, all she could do, she decided as she stepped carefully on to the floor again, was to examine the room carefully before going to bed and to be sure to lock the door. She had taken care to note, when she came up into the room earlier in the evening, that there was a key in the door. After making

the circuit of the room, therefore, looking under the bed, under the muslin-
covered hangings of the old-fashioned
dressing-table, and into the cupboards in
the wall, Nanny reached the door.

But the key had been taken away.

Small as this matter was, poor Nanny,
in her excited state, felt that she wanted
to scream on making this discovery.
Common-sense suggested that Mrs.
Bambridge's servant, having to sleep on
the ground floor in a strange house, had
taken the key in the hope that it might
fit the door of the room she was to use.
But Nanny was more in the mood for
entertaining the marvellous than the
homely and the probable, and her excited imagination pictured the unknown
and mysterious Lady Ellen as having
secreted herself about the house and

possessed herself of the key for some
purpose antagonistic to Nanny's own
comfort and repose. She felt that it
would be too childish to trouble the
occupants of the sick-room again about
what they would consider a trifle; so she
barricaded the door with a long chintz-
covered settee on casters, which stood
under one of the windows, and presently
went to bed.

She was restless, and could not sleep
for a long time. At last she fell into an
uneasy doze, troubled by feverish dreams.
A dozen times, in the course of the next
two hours, she started into wakefulness,
and lay for a few minutes a prey to
miserable imaginings before falling again
into the same unrestful slumber. At
last, having grown used to this, and
being by this time extremely sleepy, she

awoke and lay with closed eyes. The same fancies as before hung in her still half-slumbering mind : unknown voices, half-heard sounds, were troubling her. Through it all she asked herself wearily when this was going to end in sound sleep. Then the voices seemed to die away, but the other noises grew louder and more distinct; strange creakings and mumblings, and a sound like the tearing of stuff. Roused a little more, Nanny turned over on her side, and her face touched a soft, woman's hand. An attempt was at once made to withdraw this hand, but Nanny seized it, and inflicted upon it a long deep scratch with her own nails before the intruder succeeded in freeing it.

' Who's that ? who's there ?' Nanny asked with almost a shriek, as she sat up

and peered about her vainly in the darkness.

There was no answer, no sound.
Nanny leapt out of bed and ran towards
the door, but she fell over something
and rolled on the floor, hurting herself;
not so severely, however, but that the
next moment she was up again. For in
that moment of time she had heard
stealthy footsteps rapidly crossing the
room towards the door, and knew that
it was the intention of the intruder,
whose eyes had become more accustomed to the darkness than Nanny's
own, to escape under cover of. this
accident.

Nanny was a high-spirited young
woman, and could throw off her natural
feminine cowardice very effectually when
she was excited. It was the settee which

she had placed against the door over which she had fallen ; the fact that it had been displaced was proof enough, if proof were needed, that someone had entered the room. Nanny replaced it against the door with one rapid push, and stood against it, scouring the darkness with eager eyes, and remaining as motionless as possible, in order that she might hear the least movement on the part of the intruder. But for a long time she listened in vain for the slightest sound.

The complete stillness, of course, frightened her much more than even an attack would have done. Nanny even began to feel half inclined to steal out of the room and wait outside the door. But a dogged determination to get to the bottom of this mystery at all hazards conquered the suggestions of timidity. She sat down on the settee and waited.

She remained sitting motionless, and always on the watch, until the first rays of dawn began to steal through the drawn curtains of the windows. Nanny grew more uneasy as the affair seemed to grow more mysterious. She could have seen an approaching figure in the faint light which now struggled in. And she kept her eyes always in the direction of the windows, so that she might be prepared for an attack. An attack !—for Nanny did not disguise to herself her fear that it was a lunatic with whom she .had to contend.

At last, when the light had grown stronger, the strain on her staring eyes became so painful that, for one moment, Nanny had to close them. Scarcely had

she done so when, with almost inconceiv-
able rapidity, she found herself overthrown on to the ground by a rapid jerk
of the settee away from the door. Nanny
uttered a scream and a cry of ' Help !'
but by the time she had risen to her feet
certain soft sounds, growing fainter and
fainter, along the corridor towards the
staircase, told her that she had been out-
witted. She gave chase as far as the head
of the staircase, but in vain. And the
sound of the closing of a distant door,
which she believed to be the back-door
into the garden, told her that pursuit was
useless.

Sick, cold, frightened, trembling,
Nanny returned to her room. The light
was now quite strong enough for her to
see how she, watching as intently as she
had done, had in her turn been watched,

and more successfully. The bed-valance was caught up, proving that someone had been watching her from under the bed; and as the light fell full on Nanny, this 'someone' had been able to take immediate advantage of the momentary closing of the tired eyes.

The astounding agility with which the unseen watcher had crept out, pulled the settee forward, and dashed through the door was the first thing which struck Nanny with amazement and fear; then followed a momentary paralysis of terror at the thought that during all that time during which she had sat on the settee by the door, she had been under the gaze of a pair of unseen, malevolent eyes.

Whose eyes?

Nanny vowed to herself that on

the following day she would know, whatever the knowledge might cost her.

In the meantime she could not pass the rest of the night in that room by herself. She dressed hastily, and went downstairs to her husband's sick-room.

Entering softly without knocking, she found old Mrs. Ryder dozing in an armchair by the dying embers of the fire. Her head was bent forward on her breast, and she did not hear Nanny enter. Even in her agitation, the young lady could not help smiling to herself at this discovery : for in the library of petty fictions which no old lady is without, Mrs. Ryder treasured up the belief that in an armchair she could never close her eyes. Nanny glanced at the bed. Dan was lying quietly, with his eyes closed ; but

his face was flushed, and his lips moved
almost incessantly.

Nanny crept up to the bedside, and a
deep sigh escaped her as she leant wistfully over him.   Oh, he had never wit-
tingly done any harm to her, or to any
woman—Nanny was sure of that.   He
was her dear husband, her own darling
old Dan!   Nothing could alter that;
nothing *should* alter that.   Nanny found
herself saying this half aloud, with
clenched teeth.   For there was that
horrible fear at the bottom of her
heart; there was this cry always ringing in her ears: 'Lady Ellen! Lady
Ellen!'

Neither her sigh nor her whispered
words disturbed him, nor her quick-
drawn breath, as she leaned over him in
a rapture of yearning love.   When at last

she drew back, a board creaked under her tread. The sound did not rouse her husband, but old Mrs. Ryder started in her chair.

'Is it you, nurse?' she asked.

And the old lady shivered. Nanny came up to her and made her look up, blinking in the feeble light of the night-light.

'No, it is I.'

'You, child! You are not to sit up watching. Go back to bed at once. Dan would never allow it.'

'I can't go back. Whatever you say, I'm going to spend the rest of the night here,' said Nanny, with determination. 'I have had a fright; someone got into my room.'

'Into—your—room?' repeated the old lady in a troubled voice.

'Yes. We will talk about it to-morrow morning. In the meantime, I'm going to stay down here.'

The old lady looked as if she would have liked to ask some more questions ; but as the nurse, roused by their voices, now entered to take her turn at watching, Nanny escaped for the present. Taking a chair near her husband's bed-side, the young wife, now wide awake, and with her mind at its keenest, as it happens to us all during a wakeful night, thought over all the little mysteries which had already disturbed the course of her short married life, and came to a decision before morning as to what she should do. Then, as the light grew strong outside, sleep overcame her at last, and seized so firmly upon her tired senses that the nurse was able to put a

pillow under her head and a foot-
stool under her feet without rousing
her.

When she awoke it was nine o'clock.
She was full of self-reproach at first,
shamefaced and angry with herself for
her inability to watch by her husband's
side. But the nurse soothed her with
assurances that Captain Ryder was going
on quite as well as could be expected,
and that it was the consciousness of that
fact which had enabled her to sleep.
Comforted, though not convinced, Nanny
went upstairs for her morning bath.
The missing key of her bedroom-door
she found lying on the floor near the
mat outside; she would not trust it
in the lock again, but put it in her
pocket. In the breakfast-room she
found old Mrs. Ryder looking much

more aged and infirm than ever before, as a result of her share in the night's nursing.

The elder lady showed many more signs of a disturbed state of mind than the younger, eating scarcely any break-fast, and starting nervously at every sound. Nanny, indeed, felt half stupefied from the effects of violent excitement followed by heavy slumber. The poignancy of the night's terror being past, and her mind made up, she seemed even stolidly in-different, and cast scarcely a glance more than the barest courtesy demanded at her mother-in-law's face. When the old lady left the table she rose too, and was going out of the room when Mrs. Ryder stopped her.

'Antonia, my dear, I wish to speak to you.'

Nanny turned, and waited for the
next words with disconcerting passivity.
The little old lady—a little porcelain
creature she was, always dainty with old
lace and jewellery, and with a faint suggestion of lavender and pot-pourri in the
folds of her soft silk gowns—drew about
her more closely a tiny shawl of em-
broidered India muslin she was wearing,
and came up to her daughter-in-law
with the graceful movements and pretty
affected dignity of the ' keepsake ' period
to which she belonged.

' You had a fright last night, my dear,
you say. Tell me about it.'

Nanny did so at once, without hesitation or reservation. Mrs. Ryder listened
quietly, and from her manner it would
have been impossible to tell whether she
guessed who the intruder was or not.

Nanny, however, had no doubts on this point.

'It was Lady Ellen, I know,' she said, with simple conviction; 'the only questions in my mind are : whether she is sane, and what she wanted to do to me.'

'Do to you, child! You surely cannot suppose ——'

'I don't suppose she took the key out of my door, and so prepared her entrance, without some object in view. I can't tell what her object was, but I caught her hand feeling about my pillow, and I should be much more comfortable in a house where I didn't have such mysterious visitors.'

Nanny felt brave by daylight; besides, she thought she saw her way to finding a solution of the mystery. Her companion looked at her curiously.

'Of course,' said the elder lady, after a
pause, 'if such a thing were to happen
again, you would write to your father?'

'Oh no; indeed I should not!'
answered Nanny at once. 'He would
say that I had chosen of my own free will
to marry Captain Ryder, and that the
number of wives he had was therefore
my look-out.'

'Your sister Meg, then?'

'No. What could poor Meg do?
It would only make her unhappy.'

'What do you mean to do, then?'

'To find out the whole story from
someone who knows it—Mrs. Calverley.'

Into the elder lady's face there came a
faint tinge of colour.

'Mrs. Calverley? So that old busy-
body is still alive! Well, you will hear
something from her, certainly, but no one

is less likely to tell you the truth about *anything*,' she ended rather snappishly.

Through all this talk Nanny noted with astonishment and annoyance how the mystification to which she was being subjected delighted the old lady, who revelled in the perplexity on Nanny's face with a small mind's keenest enjoyment. Nanny turned abruptly and with scant courtesy to the door, impatient with such trifling, long before old Mrs. Ryder was tired of watching her puzzled face.

Carrying out the intention she had formed in the night, Nanny then ran upstairs, put on her hat, and went in search of Mrs. Calverley's house. It was a pretty, picturesque whitewashed house, with a very old roof of red pantiles, standing back a little way from the road in a nest of trees.

'And that 'ere's the Admiral—
Admiral Calverley,' said the boy who
was acting as her guide, pointing to a
rather vapid - looking blue - eyed old
gentleman in a straw hat, who was
picking snails off the dahlias in his
garden. Nanny went up to the house,
while the Admiral, who was on the
other side of a great bush of flowering
trees—lilac, laburnum, and guelder-rose,
the blossom-time of all of which was
past—disappeared into the building by a
side-door, with a transparent pretence of
not having seen her.

Nothing is so easy to understand as the
'not at home' of a servant who knows
that his mistress is in, but that she does
not wish to see the visitor. Nanny
blushed deeply, therefore, when she received this answer, and set her lips

tightly together, with her mind quite
made up that she would see this exclu-
sive old lady, and before long, too. She
knew very well that the Admiral had
seen her, and that he had gone into the
house to report upon her to his wife.

The rest of the day Nanny spent
chiefly in her husband's sick-room,
avoiding any other chance of a *tête-à-tête*
with her mother-in-law. In the meantime two of the servants she had engaged
arrived, and the desolate look the whole
house had worn began to disappear.

A little before six o'clock Charlie
Bambridge came, and Nanny, delighted
to have a chance of speaking to someone young and cheerful, went at once
to the drawing-room, and greeted him
warmly.

' My chief purpose in coming to

trouble you at a time when I'm sure you don't want to be bothered with visitors,' said he, when he had made inquiries about Captain Ryder, 'is to apologize for the barbaric conduct of— of all the rest of us the other day. There is just this excuse for the young ones,' he went on loftily, 'that Mrs. Winton, a widow who lives with her father next door to us, has taken to fertilizing her garden with fish manure, the Arabian perfume of which is so strong that she has had to buy off the objections of all the neighbours by the gift of a flowerpotful all round. My bull-dog ate up our lot, and liked it. But it didn't agree with him, and I trust that this experience will have the effect of disgusting him with foreign kickshaws. But it was inexcusable of them, all the same, to trespass upon your property, as I meant to have told you yesterday.'

The young fellow was evidently nervous, and seemed at first anxious to avoid any serious conversation. Nanny assured him, truly enough, that the ready kindness of his family had been the only bright spot, so far, in her experience of The Grange. She began to wonder why he had come. He had clearly something upon his mind, and did not know how to unburden himself of it. Nanny, who had something upon her mind, broke through their mutual reserve first.

'You were with my husband yester-day when the accident happened,' she said abruptly, when there was a pause.

'No; I came up a minute later— when I heard the crash of his fall, in

fact.   I had left him in the study, looking through some old letters and books.'

'Yes,' said Nanny quickly, 'but you
know what caused him to leap out of
the window!   You saw who it was that
startled him.   It was a woman.'

Charlie answered without looking at
her.

'Was it?   Then I give you my word
I didn't see her, Mrs. Ryder,' he said,
with so much force and appearance of
sincerity that Nanny would have believed
him but for his evident reluctance to
meet her eyes.

'You give me your word you did not
see the person whose appearance at the
window startled my husband?'

But he would not commit himself.
He reddened, stammered, and finally
said :

'Ask Captain Ryder when he gets well. I saw that he was startled, but —but really very little more. And— and as for being annoyed by inquisitive women, that was just what I came to speak about,' he went on, as if breathing more freely now that he had got on to safer ground. 'There is a meddlesome old woman whom you met at our house yesterday — Mrs. Calverley — who has been spying about here ever since she heard you were coming.'

'Yes, she was here yesterday.'

'She is always here, it seems. Now, it appears the nurse told our servant, and the girl told us, that you were frightened last night by someone, Mrs. Ryder.'

'It is quite true—I was,' said Nanny, blushing.

'Oh, you mustn't be annoyed at our hearing about it. If you ever find a blackbeetle in the dining-room, that blackbeetle will be all over the village in two hours. But I thought it was better to let you know about this old woman, so that you might circumvent her. I have no doubt it was she who frightened you, for she was lurking about outside your gates quite late last night.'

'Thank you very much for telling me,' said Nanny.

She did not attempt to undeceive the young fellow, who had evidently heard a very garbled version of the story of her fright. She thanked him for his visit, sent grateful messages to his mother and sisters, and promised him that, as soon as her husband got well, they would let him give them a row 'up the river

somewhere' in his boat. For, next to
his bulldog and his bicycle, his boat
occupied the largest share of this every-
day young man's heart.

When he had gone, Nanny put on
her hat and went out into the garden.
If this Mrs. Calverley ·was 'always
spying about,' as Charlie Bambridge had
said, she would be on the watch until
she caught her and forced her to give an
explanation of the mystery about Lady
Ellen. Nanny looked out of the princi-
pal gates, and then out of the side-gate,
but it was not until the third recon-
noitring expedition she made that evening that she at last caught sight of the
Admiral's wife walking slowly up and
down on the opposite side of the road.
It was ten o'clock and quite dark; but
as she came under the light of a gas-

lamp, Nanny recognised and ran up to her at once, and placed herself resolutely in front of the old lady, blocking the footway, determined not to be passed.

' Mrs. Calverley, I think ?' she said, in a voice which sounded timid because she was trembling so much from excitement. ' I called upon you this morning, but I was unfortunate. I was told you were not at home.'

' That, unhappily, ' is what you will always be told when you call,' answered the elder woman, in a dry, hard voice, as she looked meanwhile nervously at Nanny through a pair of gold-rimmed eye-glasses.

' Will you tell me why ?' asked Nanny, with a sob in her voice.

' I thought I had explained my reason yesterday. Knowing as I do that Cap-

tain Ryder's wife, Lady Ellen, is alive,
it is not possible for me to receive her
supplanter.'

'How do you know that Lady Ellen is
alive ?'

'By the best of all proofs.   I saw her
last night.'

'Where ?'

'Here.   She crossed the road quickly,
and went into The Grange garden by
this side-gate.'

'Did you speak to her?   Are you
sure it was she ?'

'I did not speak to her, but I am sure
it was she.   I imagine she was coming
from The White House at Bicton,
where I have seen her twice before
during the last few years.'

'The White House?   Is she insane ?
Is she locked up there ?'

' I don't know whether she is insane,
but I cannot suppose she is locked up,
for on each occasion I have seen her
going in or out. But allow me to
remind you that, sane or insane, she is
Captain Ryder's wife all the same.'

' But I want to see her—I want to see
her,' said Nanny, stamping her foot
impatiently. ' How can I believe in this
will-o'-the-wisp woman, whom everybody seems to see except me ?'

Mrs. Calverley laughed softly, and,
raising her eye-glass, began to scan
Nanny's face curiously, and not unkindly,
in the light of the gas-lamp.

' Look here, little girl,' she said at
last, ' you've been very badly treated; I
must allow that. You have married a
bad man, and you may tell him I said
so. Take my advice; now, while he is

lying ill, and can't come after you, go
away back to your friends. You will be
quite safe from him, for, when he once
suspects that you know who he is, he
won't dare to follow you. And don't
attempt to come face to face with Lady
Ellen. Although she hates her husband,
she is not at all likely to love you. And
to tell you the truth, child,' went on
Mrs. Calverley, with a sudden impulse
of expansion, ' I shan't be able to rest
till you are gone. For, knowing what a
pair of demons Dan and his wife are, I
can do nothing but haunt this place,
waiting for another tragedy, ever since I
heard that he had had the assurance to
come back.'

' Another tragedy !' echoed Nanny in
a horror-struck whisper.'

But Mrs. Calverley, already afraid

that her confidence had gone too far,
merely wished her ' Good-night ' with
her former frigidity, and hurried abruptly
away in the direction of her own home.

CHAPTER II.

Nanny's first impulse, when Mrs. Calverley left her thus abruptly, was to run
after that lady and insist on hearing
more details of the mystery of the
Ryders. But she had scarcely taken
two steps in pursuit when she stopped
short, and straightway abandoned this
intention.

After all, what was the use of it?
The Admiral's wife, with her hard voice,
her short-sighted, inquisitive stoop, and
nervous manner, was not an attractive or
sympathetic personality, and such details

as might be gathered from her lips would
come with a cold dryness which Nanny,
sensitive from recent wounds, shrank
from encountering.

The young wife said to herself that
she knew the worst Mrs. Calverley had
to tell—that Dan had been married
before, and that his first wife, Lady
Ellen, was alive. This was dreadful
enough, certainly ; but as Nanny naturally refused to believe Mrs. Calverley's
further assurances that Captain Ryder
was a bad man, and the central figure in
a ' tragedy,' she persisted in saying to
herself that there was an explanation
which would set matters right ; and this
explanation, unpleasant as it would be
to ask for it, Nanny now felt that she
must have as soon as her husband was
well enough to give it.

In the meantime the poor child felt
that life in this mystery-haunted house
was difficult.

If she could only confide in someone !
Nanny wanted to pour her story into the
sympathetic ears of kind Mrs. Bambridge, but she was restrained by a fear
lest this might include Mr. Bambridge,
and in time the boys and girls. As for
Meg, loving, devoted sister Meg, who
was sure, in spite of all her efforts, to
find out from the tone of her letters that
something was wrong, the hot tears
came fast down Nanny's cheeks at the
thought of her. Confidence in old Meg
was at this stage of affairs not to be
thought of. For Nanny knew perfectly
well what the result would be. Up
Meg would come from Edinburgh by
the next available train, in a tornado of

passion. Profiting by Captain Ryder's
illness, she would next administer a fiery-
tongued reproof to old Mrs. Ryder, as
the only representative of the family
whom she could get at; and then,
regardless of the inevitable scandal, she
would insist on carrying Nanny back
to Edinburgh without waiting to hear
Captain Ryder's version of the story,
or what he had to say in his own
defence.

So Nanny resolved, until her husband
was well, to keep her own counsel.

She got back to the house just as the
doctor was leaving it. He was holding
a conversation with old Mrs. Ryder at
the door, and Nanny was annoyed to see
on what very confidential terms they
seemed to be. She could see them,
under cover of the darkness, as they

stood in the lamp-light at the open hall-door, long before she reached it. Their voices were very low, and by their gestures it seemed that the lady was giving the doctor a long account, to which he listened assentingly.

'Yes, don't trouble yourself about him. He is going on very well. Good-night,' said he, as soon as Nanny came near enough to announce her presence with very firm steps upon the gravel.

The younger lady passed him with only a cold salutation, for, with perhaps excusable prejudice, she looked upon every friend of her mother-in-law·as her enemy.

'Dear me! where have you been, my dear?' cooed out the old lady softly, not without some apprehension in her voice. 'You shouldn't be out so late

without something round your shoulders.
You——'

' I am all right, thank you,' said
Nanny coldly.

But the gentle old lady was not the
sort of person you could avoid against
her own wish. She followed Nanny
upstairs, and asked permission to come
into her room for a moment. The
younger lady, with a wry face, had to
comply.

' I have been thinking about you, my
poor child, all the afternoon,' she bleated
out with a little sigh.

' It is very kind of you.'

' Now, don't be sarcastic with a poor
old woman. It is not like you. You
will make life too hard, my child, if
you shut up your heart against everybody who loves you and wishes you

well. Can't you learn to confide your
troubles to me, dear ? You have no
mother, and I would be a mother to
you.'

'Thank you.'

'Oh, you are hard! You forget your
husband, whom you have taken away
from me, remember; for I can't help
seeing that you have got my share of his
heart as well as your own.'

Nanny's mouth softened, and a moment's irresolution came into her pretty
eyes. The other instantly took advantage
of it.

'What does Dan care for his mother
now ? Nothing. Through you, yes,
through you, I am now all alone in the
world.'

'Oh, don't say that! I——'

'But I know it, and I don't complain.

I know very well that it is only right, and in the natural order of things, that the wife should come first. It is only when I see my poor boy in danger of being deserted by the wife he adores that my heart grows sore for him. If I were only sure—you—you would not leave him——'

The old lady, whose voice was really breaking, sank on to a chair and put a very delicate scrap of lace-edged cambric to her eyes. Her emotion was real ; the hardest thing you could say about it was that it came easily, and showed itself more easily still.

Nanny did not fall on her knees and caress her mother-in-law with the impulsive warmth she would have felt ten days before ; she moved one step nearer to her, and said curiously :

'Leave him! I am his wife, am I not? Why should I leave him?'

The old lady was for a moment rather disconcerted. Then she said half pettishly:

'Well, my dear, you have been so busy lately ferreting out old stories, that I thought perhaps you were anxious for an excuse for leaving him.'

'Ferreting—out—old—stories!' repeated Nanny slowly, while an indignant flush rose in her cheeks. 'I think, considering what I have learnt from one person and another, I might be excused if I did want to do a little "ferreting," as you call it. But I don't intend to try. I am going to wait until Dan is well, and then tell him everything that I have heard, and ask him to explain it all. I can trust my husband.'

This was a brave speech, as the resolution of which it was the fruit had been hard to make. But old Mrs. Ryder did not seem to see the trust and self-sacrifice it implied. She remained sitting with her tiny pocket-handkerchief in her hands, while an expression of annoyance and perplexity came over her features.

'And when he gets well—you will tell him—what will you tell him? Why not leave these old stories alone?'

'I can't—I can't,' broke out Nanny passionately, out of patience with the old lady's demands. 'I shouldn't be human if I could be satisfied with knowing just what I do and no more. Why, I don't even know whether—— '

'Sh! sh!' hissed old Mrs. Ryder, glancing around her nervously. 'There are servants in the house now, remember,

new servants, all eyes and ears. Now
listen,' and she dropped her voice till it
was scarcely louder than a whisper: 'I
have something to tell you—about Dan.'
She paused, and drew her handkerchief
across her lips, which were dry and
parched through her excitement. 'He
will be about again before long, we hope.
But,' and she raised her eyes in pleading
terror to her daughter-in-law's face, 'it
will be months before he is quite himself.
The doctor thinks this illness—will affect
his mind—his memory—and that unless
he is kept very quiet and free from all
excitement — he   may   never .wholly
recover, but remain in a half-childish
state—for the rest—of his life !'

Nanny, white even to her lips, received this announcement in dead silence.
Then came a moment of doubt.   She

looked nervously at her mother-in-
law.

' The doctor told you this, you say?'

' When he had heard what I had to
tell him about his life in India—yes.'

Nanny drew a long breath.

' I see. Thank you. Don't tell me
any more!'

The poor child put her hands to her
ears. She felt she could not bear another
word. Her mother-in-law had the sense
to recognise this; and quietly, in a
shame-faced sort of way, as if remorseful
for having had to deal such blows, she
went away.

There was happily, as in most women
who are good for anything, a strong practical side to Nanny's nature. Having
once said to herself that she would do
nothing and say nothing in the matter of

the family secret until her husband was
well enough to be consulted, she devoted
herself to nursing him, taking her share
of waiting and watching with her mother-
in-law and the nurse, and found by so
doing a time-worn relief from her
troubles.   In the intervals of nursing she
made a systematic inspection of the house
from garret to cellar, animated partly by
girlish delight at having a home of her
own, and partly by the nascent house-
wifely instinct, which told her that
something more ought to be done to it to
bring it up to date.

   Two days after that final scene with
her mother-in-law, since which Nanny
had resolutely declined to reopen the old
subject with her, the young mistress of
The Grange was sitting on the wide,
shallow stairs which led from the first to

the second or attic story, surveying with a meditative and distasteful air a vast expanse of wall on her left covered with paper of that singular pattern known to our immediate ancestors as ' marbled.'

' Why " marbled"?' asked Nanny with a shake of the head, addressing Laura Bambridge, who was laboriously winding up a piece of string with which the two ladies had been measuring the exact length of the gallery for an ' art ' wallpaper.

For the lads and lasses at Brent Lodge were still Nanny's chief consolation, and each day she found some excuse for having at least one of them to share her loneliness.

' For that matter, why " art"?' retorted Laura. ' It doesn't really want more imagination to see a likeness to blocks of

marble in those prosaic blue zigzags on a
butter-coloured ground than to see the
connection between art and a pattern of
pink cauliflower. Our papas and mammas
read Byron and Tom Moore, and liked to
fancy themselves living in marble palaces.
We go to South Kensington and imagine
ourselves "artistic." And all the time
we are just the same stodgy old Britons
underneath it all.'

'You are severe and misanthropical
this morning,' said Nanny, laughing.

'I am consumed by a sense of the
vanity of all things, just because I can't
get my own particular "wanity," as
Mr. Weller says,' admitted Laura. 'We
can't get papa to see that, in order to
carry out the great principle of "the
survival of the fittest," our sealskin
jackets absolutely must be "done up"

for this winter. He says this "doing up" costs so much; that we had better throw the sealskins aside and make our old cloth coats do instead. Now, what is the use of training us up to appreciate scientific theories if we are not allowed to put them in practice?'

'It's very hard,' said Nanny. 'If I had known you to be smarting under the sense of such an injustice, I would not have asked you to come and share my woes about wall-paper.'

'Never mind,' said Laura, with an exaggerated sigh. 'In the contemplation of your sorrows I can forget my own.'

And she skipped along the gallery towards Nanny so quickly that she tripped in a hole in the worn carpet, and was thrown head-foremost against the wall at the end. To the surprise of both, the wall yielded a little, and the despised marble paper cracked.

'What have I done?' cried poor Laura. 'I thought this was the outer wall. Surely my head isn't hard enough to make a passage through into the garden.'

They both began to laugh with the immoderate merriment one can enjoy at twenty, even with a mysterious secret hanging over one's head. And both began to tap on the wall and to examine it.

'I thought it was the outer wall, too,' said Nanny, as they discovered beyond a doubt, by the sound their knuckles made on the wall, that there was a hollow space behind it. 'But now, of course, I remember that there is an attic above this corner, and—yes, the study is right underneath. Then there must be a room or a space behind here : the question is, how to get at it. There is certainly no door from the inside, unless, indeed '—and she began to feel more carefully —' there has been one here and it has been blocked up.'

She tore a small piece of the paper off, enough to show that behind there was a wall of lath and plaster. They had just discovered this when they caught sight of old Mrs. Ryder at the other end of the gallery. She had just come upstairs.

' The old lady looks scared ; she thinks we're pulling the house down,' whispered Laura, under cover of stooping to pick up her handkerchief.

She *did* look scared. Nanny ran to

meet her, afraid that something had gone
wrong.

'What's the matter, mamma? Has
anything happened?'

'No, dear, no. I don't grow any
younger, and the stairs try me. That's
all. What are you girls doing up here?'
she continued, as she shook hands with
Laura.

'I want to have a new paper on the
wall here, as soon as Dan gets well,' said
Nanny. 'This is so dreadfully ugly and
common-looking, isn't it?'

'That is what you young people
think of everything chosen by. your
elders, I suppose,' answered the old lady,
with as near an approach to tartness as
her general amiability permitted.

There was a pause. The young ladies
both felt snubbed. As a diversion,

Laura again tapped on the hollow-sounding wall.

'There seems to be a bit of wasted space here that we can't account for,' she said lightly.

'Yes, mamma, is there a room there, do you know? And if so, where is the door?'

'There is no room,' answered the old lady quietly. 'This is the east end of the house, and it was a fancy of my poor husband's that by having a double wall we should be protected against the east winds. That is all.'

'What a strange idea! And what a pity to give so much space up to it!' exclaimed Laura.

'It is not much—not more than a couple of feet.' A shadow passed upon the old lady's face. Evidently she did

not care for her late husband's whims
to be laughed at. She hastened to
change the conversation, and assuming
a more conciliatory tone towards the
views of the young people, she continued : 'Perhaps this paper is rather
ugly; though, having been used to it
years ago, I did not look at it with your
æsthetically cultivated eyes.'

'Then you won't be offended if I
have it repapered, mamma ?'

'Of course not, my dear. This is
your home now, not mine; you can do
whatever you like in it. But if you will
take my advice, instead of repapering
the wall, you will hang it with curtains
all the way up the stairs. That will be
more modern still.'

'Oh, that would be lovely ! But
wouldn't it be frightfully expensive ?'

'Not if you have printed cotton
curtains, I think. I am going up to
town this afternoon, you know. Shall
I call at Liberty's, and see what they
would come to?'

'Oh, if you would, mamma! What
is the length, Laura?'

'Here is the string, with a knot in it
at each end of the exact length. It is
not exactly what you would call scientific
measurement, I'm afraid; but we couldn't
find a yard measure.'

'The worst of it is,' remarked Nanny,
with a touch of gloom, 'that if the
curtains *do* prove too expensive, we shall
have missed an afternoon's enjoyment.
Laura's brother Arthur has a half-holiday
to-day, and we were going to buy some
paper in the village, and make him turn
paper-hanger.'

'It would have been such fun,' added
Laura wistfully.

'But amateur paper-hanging would
never answer. It is very difficult indeed
to do properly,' said old Mrs. Ryder
quickly. 'Look, Nanny. If you will
promise to leave the wall alone till I
come back I will bring you the curtains,
whatever they cost. If they cost more
than you think Dan would approve of
your spending, I'll pay half of the money
myself.'

'Oh, how good of you! But I don't
like to——'

'Yes, yes, I should like to get them.
I want to see the old house look nice.
Only—don't meddle with the wall till I
come back.'

'No. We promise,' said Nanny.

'Will you come downstairs with me

now, and see me to the station ? And I suppose, Nanny, you mean to spend the rest of the time in Dan's room ?'

The younger ladies followed her downstairs, and after luncheon, which was just served, they accompanied her to the station.

As soon as the train had started, however, sharp-eyed Laura pursed her mouth up knowingly, and said :

' Now, I wonder if that dear old lady imagines that we don't see through her little artifice ! She wouldn't have been so fond of our society if she had not wanted to keep us out of mischief, and she hoped that by the time she had started we should have forgotten all about that wall.'

' Yes. She didn't want us to paper it,

did she ?' said Nanny doubtfully. 'I
wonder why !'

'*I* know. She wanted us to leave
that wall alone because there *is* a room
behind it, which she doesn't want us to
see into. And of course, as long as
human nature remains what it is, that is
the very way to make us want to see.'

Nanny stopped short, and stared at
the girl as if she had received a great
shock.

'Oh !' she gasped. 'You don't think
that, do you ?'

'Don't take it so tragically,' cried
Laura, laughing. 'There's a room that
somebody or other would like to block
up in every old house, you may be sure
of that. And Mrs. Ryder, being a
woman of strong will, has had her own
way about it. Most likely it is the

room in which her husband died,' she
added in a graver tone.

'Very likely,' assented Nanny with
surprising eagerness. For Laura could
not know what a load of irritating
mystery the young wife had had to bear
already. 'I never thought of that. I
wonder if there is a room there!' she
added after a pause.

'It is very easy to find out,' cried
Laura, with girlish eagerness for the
undertaking. 'The old plan — you
know. Put a handkerchief, or a book,
or a flower, anything, in every window,
and then see from the outside whether
there's a window left out.'

'Ye—es, we might do that,' said
Nanny hesitatingly.

'Do, do let us do it! It will be such
fun! It is your own house, you know,

though I dare say that old lady doesn't
mean it to be so any more than she can
help. At any rate, there can be no harm
in finding out about the windows—can
there ?'

' No—o, I suppose not.'

So it was settled that a book, being a
heavy thing which the breeze could not
blow away, should be placed in every
window ; and when they reached The
Grange, Laura forced the still half-reluc-
tant Nanny to carry out the plan. Before
they had half finished their task, Arthur
Bambridge, who had been invited by
Nanny the day before, arrived and entered with great zest into the occupation
on hand. That is to say, he stood in
the garden and directed them from point
to point in a hoarse whisper, which was
supposed to be less irritating to the nerves

of a convalescent man than speech uttered
in a natural voice. Nanny, however, had
ascertained that her husband was asleep
before joining in this dubious frolic.

At last the task was done ; and the
two ladies stood together at the window
in front of which old Mrs. Ryder had
found them that morning. Nanny was
shaking like a leaf as they put their heads
out, and saw Arthur standing on the
grass below trying to prop a ladder
against the wall. His face was flushed
with boyish excitement, although he
affected a manner which was a cross between that of the bored man-about-town
and that of the scientific investigator.

' What are you doing ?' sobbed out
Nanny in a frightened voice.

Laura turned round quickly to look at
her. The young wife's hands hung down

at her sides ; her face was wet and cold.

' Oh, you are ill ! You have got too much excited about this nonsense,' cried Laura.

Nanny shook her head.

' Stop him,' she whispered.

Laura put her head out of the window, and frantically made signs to her brother, who had already ascended two or three rungs of the ladder, to go down again. Recovering herself, Nanny too looked out and smiled faintly at the astonished lad.

' Wait till I come down,' she said, after clearing her throat with difficulty ; ' I want to go up first.'

She knew that she was very foolish to be so much moved without cause, and by the time she and her companion got

down into the garden she had recovered
herself sufficiently to laugh almost
naturally at her own fright.

Still, the sight of two empty windows
at the end of the house, with the thin-
ning trails of Virginia creeper swinging
gently in front of them, filled her again
with alarm which she could not have
explained away to her companions without letting them into the secret of the
shock she had already suffered in that
house. Arthur was looking very cross ;
he was not old enough to be very chivalrous, and he put down her desire to
go first to ' feminine nastiness,' and to
jealousy of his masculine superiority.

' All right,' he said rather haughtily ;
' of course you can go first if you like, Mrs.
Ryder; but don't blame me if there's a stray
rat, or cat, or bat in the room that flies out

at you and gives you a fright. I can't catch
you if you fall down, you know; for I
shall be holding the ladder.'

'You are not very courteous, Arthur,'
said his sister reprovingly.

'Never mind. I shall be all right,'
said Nanny.

And seeing there was no help for it,
and being herself on fire with curiosity,
she at once began the ascent of the ladder,
in spite of the expostulations of Laura,
who was afraid that she might faint.

'Here's something to pull back the
catch of the window with, Mrs. Ryder,'
said Arthur, handing her his pocket-
knife.

Nanny got up the ladder nimbly and
neatly enough, having been 'a bit of a
tomboy,' as her nurse used to say, and
not disdainful of the art of tree-climbing.

She opened the pocket-knife, drew back
the window-catch, and with some difficulty raised the sash. Then she turned
round to look down, with a white,
excited face.

' It is a room,' she whispered. ' I'm
going to get in.'

Laura began to remonstrate, frightened
by her paleness. But Arthur 'shut his
sister up ' with a remark of curt brother-
liness, delivered in an undertone. When
they looked up again, Nanny had disappeared inside the room. There were a
few moments for the two people below
of breathless, delicious excitement. Then
young Mrs. Ryder reappeared at the
window.

Nay, was it young Mrs. Ryder? A
creature with haggard, ghastly face,
starting eyes, and shaking white lips,

who made signs to the two below, but without speaking.

'Go up to her, or let me go up to her, Arthur! She must not come down this way alone, at any rate,' whispered Laura, much shocked.

But Nanny had caught the words, and, before either could mount one step, she was out on the ladder, shutting the window with a sudden accession of nervous force.

'Don't come! don't come!' she cried in a firm voice. 'I will come down.'

CHAPTER III.

I⊤ was quite clear to both Laura and
Arthur Bambridge that something she
had seen in the long-concealed room had
given young Mrs. Ryder a terrible shock.
She came down the ladder firmly, but
very slowly, and quick-witted Laura
wondered whether she had seen something she did not wish to speak about,
and was trying to invent some story to
account for the fright she had evidently
received.

This, in truth, was the case. Nanny,
sick at heart and terror-struck, knew she

must not confess what had frightened
her, and yet shrank from telling an
absolute falsehood. Arthur, who was
entirely lacking in his sister's delicate
perception, helped her out of her difficulty by his first question.

'Well, Mrs. Ryder, you were boasting
the other day that you didn't believe in
ghosts, that you were never frightened
unless there was real reason for fear,
and——'

'There was real reason for fear,' said
Nanny, plucking up spirit to answer
him. 'You might have run away with
the ladder.'

'It wasn't that fear that made you look
so frightened. You've only just thought
of that. Now, what was it really?'

'A cat, or a rat, or a bat, Mr. Inquisitive.'

'Now, Mrs. Ryder, you're only putting me off. I shall go up and see for
myself.'

Nanny's face changed, and she laid
her hand on his arm to restrain him;
while his sister, with less ceremony,
pulled the ladder away from the wall,
and so shook him off.

'Why mayn't I go up? Why mayn't
I go up?' asked he eagerly, like a spoilt
child. 'If there are really rats there,
let me get Harrison's terrier—Harrison,
the blacksmith, has a first - rate ratter,
and——'

'Really, Arthur, you don't suppose
Mrs. Ryder wants all the village ringing
with the exciting story of a rat-hunt at
The Grange!'

Arthur was about to answer in a lofty
tone of offended dignity, for he con-

sidered himself to stand on a more
elevated plane of refinement than Laura
did. But Nanny broke in with a very
gentle voice :

'A terrier would be of no use, Arthur,
because I don't even know that there are
any rats. That room is only a lumber-
room.'

'But something frightened you!
Lumber wouldn't frighten you — old
boxes and things like that.'

'Lumber did frighten me, you see.
Now, don't go about telling everybody
that I went into hysterics at the sight
of a few boxes piled on one another,
or they will say that Mrs. Ryder has a
bad conscience, and that there is something wrong at The Grange.'

But she could not quite keep up the
light tone she had assumed. Her face

quivered at the last words. Then she caught Laura's eye, and saw that the girl's face was full of kindness and sympathy, whereupon she had to turn away abruptly to hide her tears.

' Let us go in,' she said ; ' it is getting cold.'

But it was not cold ; although it was late October, the sun was bright and warm. Laura frowned and nodded energetically at her brother to signify to that obtuse youth that he was to second her in what she was going to say ; and then she told Nanny that they had to be home early, and marched Arthur off before that young gentleman had made up his mind in what manner to show his displeasure at the liberties which were being taken with him.

They left Nanny on the lawn, under

the cedar-trees, and there she remained,
quite benumbed and helpless under the
fresh blow which had fallen upon her,
with eyes which had lost their capacity
for seeing anything but those long-shut-
up windows and the secret behind them.
And yet what had she seen? Nothing
but a pile of lumber, as she had truly
told her light-hearted companions of
a few minutes before. But then it was
lumber which told a tale, and a ghastly
tale. Nanny saw the apartment now
as plainly as she had done ten minutes
ago; smelt again the mouldy, close
smell of a chamber long shut up from
the outer air.

It had been a bedroom, and in use at
the time when it was suddenly closed.
A large washhand-stand stood in one
corner, with a piece of dried-up soap

in the uncovered soap-dish, and traces of water in the displaced jug and in the washhand - basin. Everything else in the room was in confusion—not the confusion of accident or of neglect, but the evident result of a mad access of passion. Pictures had been torn from the walls, and lay, the frames shattered, the glass almost powdered, on the ground. A chest of drawers had been overthrown, and the contents, deep in the dust of many years, lay in a heap, with a broken looking-glass on the top of all. The window-curtains had been torn down, the mantelpiece ornaments swept off. But all this formed only the blurred background to a picture which Nanny felt that nothing would ever obliterate from her mind. The bed, one of the old - fashioned mahogany erections of

which there were many more in the
house, had been dragged into the middle
of the room, and was the most con-
spicuous object in it. The bed-clothes
had disappeared, or lay lost among the
disordered heaps of clothing on the
floor. But the paillasse remained, pre-
senting a spectacle so horrible that
Nanny grew cold at the recollection,
for it was dyed with a stain which spread
down the side of the bedstead and over
a wide space of the carpet, and dis-
coloured by time and the accumulation
of dust as it was, Nanny knew that it
showed where there had once been a
pool of blood.

This awful discovery had shocked her
so much that the thought of penetrating
into a second and larger room beyond,
the door of which was kept open by a

fallen chair, had not even occurred to
her. Her one idea had been to escape
from the sight, and to hide it from the
others. Now, left to herself, however,
she half wished she had gone further in
her researches. What could she have
learnt, indeed, to lessen the horror of
what she knew? Might not even uncertainty be better than certainty? For
conjecturing busily in spite of herself,
there came a horrible suspicion into the
poor young wife's mind. A crime had
been committed in the shut-up room.
Was it murder? With new meaning,
a half-forgotten sentence in the letter
Meg had written to her on first hearing
of her engagement to Dan came back to
her mind, about a certain Ralph Ryder
of Brent of evil reputation. And then
Mrs. Calverley had talked of a tragedy.

But how to reconcile this with what she knew of Dan, the kindest and most devoted of husbands, the gentlest and most chivalrous of men? Could even madness change a man so much?

She started guiltily on hearing the trail of a woman's skirt over the grass. It was the nurse, who came up to her with a smiling face.

'You look as if you wanted some good news, ma'am, and I've brought it,' she said. 'The Captain's woke up quite sensible, and much better, and he says would you please come and see him. I had half a mind to tell him you were out, because he wants to talk, and he didn't ought to excite himself yet. But he seemed so wistful, I hadn't the heart. You'll be careful, and not let him talk too much, will you, ma'am?'

Nanny promised, and returned to the house with the nurse very slowly. Mrs. Walters, who had been shrewd enough to discover that there was a skeleton in The Grange cupboard, and who, of course, took the part of the submissive young lady against the strong-willed one, ventured on another remark.

'I'm glad old Mrs. Ryder isn't here just now, when the poor gentleman is able to talk sensible for the first time,' she said, with a sidelong look.

'Yes, I would rather have his first words myself,' assented Nanny discreetly.

'I shouldn't wish to say anything disrespectful of her,' went on the nurse. 'But I don't hold with worrying people when they're ill, and I'm sure the way that old lady used to hang over his bed, listening to his words when he was not himself,

must have worried Captain Ryder, even
though he didn't not to say know what
was going on.'

'Yes, yes, I've thought so too,' said
the young wife. 'And there was
nothing to listen to. There was nothing
important in what he said.'

There was a half-questioning inflec-
tion in her voice. Mrs. Walters
answered promptly :

'Nothing whatever. It was mostly
all about you, ma'am. Only once——'

'Well ?'

The nurse hesitated, and then went
on with her speech, believing, good
soul ! that she was giving the pretty
young lady a useful warning. This
seemed the more probable that Nanny's
face was full of excitement and interest
immediately.

'Once he did say something about a
letter.' Nanny stopped short, but then,
recovering herself, went on, tottering in
her walk. She made a sign to the nurse
to go on. 'Some wicked letter that
somebody must have written to him
about you, ma'am, I think, for he
seemed afraid that they would take you
away from him. He seemed in a
dreadful state about it, and old Mrs.
Ryder didn't seem to like it. I dare say
she is a little jealous of his being so fond
of you. Mothers mostly are of their
sons' wives: don't you think so, ma'am?'

'Yes, I suppose so,' answered Nanny
mechanically.

She entered the sick-room like a
mouse. The curtains of one window
had been drawn back, and the light fell
through the white blind on Captain

Ryder's pale face. He looked so dif-
ferent without the sunburn, so old and
worn and gray, that the discrepancy
between the age he owned to and the
age he looked struck Nanny with
overwhelming force. And if he had
deceived her in that one particular, why
not in others?

In the very moment that this thought
occurred to her she was seized with
remorse. For the look on her husband's
face as he held out his arms touched her
to the quick.

'Nanny, my darling!' he said in a
weak voice.

And the next moment he was holding
her head between his trembling hands,
devouring her little flower-face with
eyes luminous with tenderness.

'Oh, Nanny, I can't talk to you,

child. I—I shall make a fool of myself
if I do. It is horrible to be ill, Nanny,
and to feel that you are a long way away
from—from the creature you want—that
you are always going farther—farther—
that something—somebody is drawing
you away. I want you to stay by me,
little one. Don't let me feel it again.
Don't tremble, child ; don't look frightened. Somebody—my mother, I think
it was—always seemed to be coming
between you and me, whispering to me,
and—what was it I wanted to say ? I
—I can't remember.'

His head, which he had raised from
the pillow, fell back upon her shoulder.
The exertion had made his face moist,
and caused his breath to come quickly.
Nanny was moved to tears ; she was
frightened also, both by his physical con-

dition and by his last words.   What was
it he wanted to remember ?

For a few happy moments, with his
head in her arms, he forgot the thought
which had been worrying him.   But
suddenly he looked up again.

'Nanny,' he said, in a husky, weak
voice, scanning her face with wistful
eyes, 'what was it?   Can't you help
me to remember what it was?   My
head seems confused still — and —
and——'

'Don't try to remember,' whispered
Nanny, alarmed both by what he half
remembered and by what he wholly
forgot.   'Don't think of anything until
you are stronger, except *me*.'

With a sigh which seemed to shake
his weak frame, he looked up in her face,
and passed his trembling hand over the

hair which fell in little silky rings over her forehead.

'Not think of anything except you? Oh, Nanny, you need not tell me that! Whether the dreams I had were pleasant or unpleasant, they were always of you— —you—nothing but you.'

'You mustn't have unpleasant dreams about me,' said Nanny, smiling.

'No, dear, no. I need not dream about you at all now that I can have you beside me. But——'

He paused, and his wife saw, by the look which came over his face, that his thoughts were going back again to the subject which had been worrying him. He frowned painfully, as if trying to recollect lost impressions, and at last, in spite of her entreaties that he would not trouble himself about anything until

he was quite well, he seized her left
hand, and, clasping it tightly in his,
said :

' Tell me, Nanny, have you seen anything about the house—to trouble you,
or—or perplex you, while I have been
lying here ?   Have you seen—or fancied
you have seen—any *person* who, according to all reason, *could not have been
there ?*   Answer me, Nanny — answer
me !'

But for a few moments she could not.
Her lips were parched, her tongue seemed
powerless, while her head swam with
wild conjectures.   At last, however, she
seemed to understand.   He had believed
Lady Ellen to be dead, and he had seen
her alive.   Nanny's breath came fast.
She threw a rapid glance at her husband's
face, saw how excited he was, and,

remembering the nurse's warning, resolved at all hazards to keep her fears
and her fancies from him for the present.
Fortunately, too, she could say with
truth she had not *seen* anyone.

'Answer me, dear,' repeated Captain
Ryder.

'No, Dan, I have not seen anybody,'
she said simply at last. 'But if I had,
I shouldn't let you talk about it now,
dear.'

He smiled at her and pressed her hand
to his lips. He believed her, but yet he
did not seem satisfied.

'I think, Dan,' she suggested gently,
'that you had ugly fancies when you —
you were ill — a sort of nightmare, in
fact. But now you're getting well, and
you won't have them any more.'

For a moment he was silent, looking

at her fixedly.   At last he spoke in a
hesitating, uncertain manner.

' I suppose you are right; I had
fancies because I was ill.   And yet '
—again his eyebrows contracted, and the
look of perplexity came back into his
eyes—' I felt so sure that it was before
my accident I saw——'

Nanny watched his lips eagerly, wondering whether he was going to confess.
But, after a pause, he only added, in
a dreamy tone : ' What I saw.'

There was silence for a few minutes.
Captain Ryder seemed to be struggling
with his dim recollections ; Nanny was
afraid to speak : afraid, on the one hand,
to allow him to excite himself by this
talk—anxious, on the other hand, for him
to utter just the few words which would
make his whole meaning clear.   A bell

rang somewhere, and husband and wife looked at each other in a startled manner.

'My mother, I suppose,' remarked Captain Ryder, in a tone of some annoyance.

At the name Nanny, as if caught in some guilty act, tried to withdraw herself from her husband's arms; but he instantly fell into a paroxysm of excitement, and detaining her with all the force he could use, he stammered out:

'No, no, no! That is just what I knew, what I felt, what I feared! She is standing between you and me, Nanny; she has some secret which she is holding over our heads. Sometimes I feel that I hate her——'

'Oh, hush! don't say such things,

Dan,' cried Nanny, terribly alarmed by
the wildness of his words, and by the
glow which excitement was bringing into
his cheeks and into his eyes; for it
seemed to the poor child that the passion
she was stirring made the crime which
she suspected seem more probable. She
had never seen him so angry before, and
her fears made the sight of his frowning
face a torture to her.

'I don't think it is mamma, Dan,' she
said at last, in a timid voice. 'She
would have been in here by this time.
Let me go and see who it is.'

She drew herself away, and had
reached the door, when she was startled
by Dan's voice.

'I know!' he cried, in tones much
stronger than before. 'Someone was
with me—a young fellow; yes, Bam-

bridge ! Send for young Bambridge,
Nanny ; he saw what I did.'

' Very well, dear, I will,' said his wife,
as she left the room.

One of the maids met her in the hall.

' A gentleman is in the drawing-room
who wishes to see you, ma'am,' said the
girl.

' One of the young Mr. Bambridges ?'
asked Nanny.

' No, ma'am. Mr. Eley, he said his
name was.'

Valentine Eley! Nanny made her
way to the drawing-room slowly, not at
all anxious to see this gentleman who
held the Ryder secret, whatever it was,
as a marketable commodity.

The big drawing-rooms were almost
dark when Nanny reached them. The
household not being yet in full working

order, the lamps had not been brought in. The moment she entered, almost before she was well inside the room, in fact, the young man rushed impulsively towards her, and said :

'Oh, Mrs. Ryder, my sister wants to know if she may leave Teddington and come up to The White House.'

It was plain that in the darkness Valentine, expecting to meet old Mrs. Ryder, had taken it for granted that he was in her presence. Nanny, not anxious to undeceive him yet, sank at once on to a seat, lest her height should betray her.

The young man, who was evidently much excited, babbled on at breakneck pace :

'You know that Captain Ryder has been ill, and that after an illness he always

has one of these attacks, when nobody
can manage him but my sister. Well,
he is sure, living so near, to come straight
back to The White House again when
the fit comes on ; and then what am I to
do ? The Captain is strong enough to
murder me, and, without being a coward,
one may dislike the prospect. You
see——'

Valentine stopped short. His eyes
having now grown accustomed to the
gloom, he had perceived his mistake,
and was overcome with consternation.

'I suppose it was the other Mrs.
Ryder, old Mrs. Ryder, whom you
wished to see?' said Nanny quietly.

'Yes—er—it was ; certainly it was. I
should never have thought of troubling
you, though I suppose,' he went on, with
some hesitation, 'it is not indiscreet to

infer that you know all about the—the
Ryder secret, as I may call it?'

'I know something of it, certainly,'
she answered in a dull voice.

Valentine was silent for a few moments. He had the wit to guess that
she did not know everything, cool as she
was, and he was wondering how far his
own indiscretion had enlightened her,
and whether it would be to his advantage
to let her know still more than she did.
He decided not to tell her the whole
truth, but to make a bid for her gratitude
by pretending to do so.

'Pray don't think me impertinent,' he
began, 'when I say that I think you are
being very unfairly treated. If the affair
could have been kept from your knowledge altogether, I should have said:
"Keep it from her by all means." But

since something was bound to leak out, it would have been much fairer to do at first what I propose to do now—make you fully acquainted with all the details of the story.'

Nanny, who, with youthful timidity, had sat down, thus allowing him to take a seat also, sprang upon her feet again. She could not risk hearing allegations against her husband from the lips of this creature.

'Excuse me, Mr. Eley,' she said, in a trembling voice, but full of passion and fire; 'I cannot hear them. I do know there is a secret, and I dare say you know more of it than I do. But, as you only learned it by accident, you have no right to communicate it to anyone else.'

'But if they are wronging you in keeping you in ignorance?'

Nanny shook her head, at first unable to speak in answer, since this suggestion seemed to point unmistakably in the direction of her worst fears.

' I will wait until my husband is well enough to tell me himself,' she said.

Valentine Eley came a step nearer to her.

' But your husband doesn't know as much as I do,' said he in a low voice.

Nanny turned upon him quickly.

' Doesn't he know that his first wife is alive ?' she exclaimed.

Valentine paused before answering discreetly :

' All I said was that Captain Ryder doesn't know as much as I do.'

' Well,' Nanny answered with spirit, ' he shall find it out as soon as he gets well, and then we will get rid of the

army of blackmailers together, whatever
it may cost.'

' Oh,' said Valentine, quite coolly, and
with no trace of indignation at her
uncivil suggestion, ' if all the world
knows, it won't cost much. Only a
length of rope to one member of the
family, and a consequent shock to the
feelings of the rest. Good-evening. I
am so sorry to have intruded upon you.'

He was quite easy, quite happy, and
seemed unconscious that his conduct was
at all open to question, as he smiled
upon his hostess with benignant blue
eyes, and bowed himself out with a
sidelong look at a mirror in which it
was too dark for him to see more than
the outline of his figure.

Nanny remained where he- had left
her for nearly an hour, until she heard

another ring at the outer bell, and ran
out into the hall.   As she had expected,
the arrival was old Mrs. Ryder, whose
face fell at sight of her.

'I've brought the curtains, dear,' said
the old lady with nervous haste.

'Oh, have you?' said Nanny.

'Yes, dear; I got them at a shop in
Oxford Street, where they are selling off,
and they were *so* cheap.'

'That's right, thank you.   Thank
you very much.'

'How is Dan, dear?' went on the old
lady, fidgeting with some small parcels,
and not looking her daughter-in-law in
the face.

'Oh, he's—he's much better.   He
has been awake a long time.   We've
been talking.'

The old lady started.   After a minute

more, passed in fumbling among her
purchases, she said :

'Talking ! Not—not about anything
too exciting, I hope ?'

'No Wh.it I have to say that is
exciting I kept for you.'

It was a challenge. Standing upright,
the old lady turned to her.

'What do you mean, dear ?' she asked
falteringly.

'Are you going upstairs ? If you are,
I will go with you, if I may.'

Without another word they went upstairs, but, on reaching old Mrs. Ryder's
bedroom-door, Nanny passed it and
went straight on to the end of the
corridor, where the built-up door was.

'I found out to-day,' she said quietly,
'that there is a room behind here.'

In the few moments of silence which

followed, she could hear the silk dress the old lady wore rustling as she stood.

' Well,' she said at last, ' that is not a great discovery.'

' And I found out why it is shut up. There was a murder committed there.'

The old lady staggered, taken utterly off her guard. Turning sharply upon her daughter-in-law, she faltered out in a terror-stricken whisper :

' *Who told you ?*'

CHAPTER IV.

NANNY received very quietly her mother-in-law's involuntary confession. For it was a confession. The vehement words, ' Who told you ?' forced out of her in a moment of terror, could not be explained away. Old Mrs. Ryder felt this, and she walked to the nearest window with tottering feet, pushed up the sash, and leaned out, with her drawn face exposed to the night air, and to a fine rain which had just begun to fall.

' You will get wet,' said Nanny, very gently.

She felt a pang of pity for this fragile-looking old lady, who had borne the weight of a hideous secret for years and years.

The old lady started back, and for a moment Nanny thought, as the wrinkled face appeared to soften under the gaze of her sympathetic eyes, that her mother-in-law was going to do the only wise and honest thing, and to tell her frankly the whole story. But the habits of a quarter of a century are not broken through in a moment; she was secretive by nature, as most women are, and her tendency to undue reserve, instead of being checked by an intelligent modern education, had been fostered by years of brooding over a tragic story. She seemed to withdraw into herself again as she wrapped the long black velvet cloak she wore more

closely round her, and drew a gentle,
affected little sigh.   All hope of her confidence was over.

'There really was something dreadful
done in that room many years ago, I
believe,' she said, without again meeting
Nanny's eyes.   'But I need not tell you,
my dear, that we don't talk about it.
You may guess how old the story is
when I say that Dan has never even
heard of it; and I particularly beg you—
though to a woman of your sense it is
scarcely necessary to insist on this—not
to mention it to him.'

And so the matter ended, old Mrs.
Ryder walking back to her room as if
there was no more to be said, Nanny
returning, restless and unsatisfied, to her
husband's room.

For the next few days the young wife

was chiefly occupied by the delights
attending her husband's gradual return
to health and strength.   There was the
excitement of his sitting up in bed for
the first time.   Next followed the enjoyment of seeing him in a chair.   And last
of all came the pleasure of lending him
the support of her arm when he left the
sick-room for the first time.   Not that
he needed this support.   Captain Ryder
was not much pulled down by his illness,
and   recovered   quickly.   But   Nanny
liked   to   think   that   he   wanted   her
help.

Old Mrs. Ryder had kept out of her
daughter-in-law's way since the day on
which the latter had discovered the shut-
up room.   The only event which had
broken the monotony of these few days
had been a formal call on the part of the

Vicar. The Reverend George Melladew was a Broad Churchman, with no more salient characteristic than a tendency to let all the work of the parish slip out of his own hands and into those of his curates, except on such occasions as a smart wedding or grand funeral, when he would conduct the service himself, to the admiration of all the old ladies, who thought much more of him than they would have done of a man weaker of voice, but stronger in the Christian virtues. Nanny found him rather a stilted, dry sort of person, and felt more awkward and girlish in his society than she had done since her marriage. She felt annoyed with herself, and expressed a fear to her husband that the Vicar had found her stupid.

When, however, Mrs. Bambridge and

two of the girls called, two days later,
they said that Mr. Melladew had called
her a charming woman.

' He didn't seem charmed,' said Nanny
dubiously. ' He kept letting the conversation drop, and as I wasn't clever
enough to pick it up again, and Dan
wouldn't talk at all, most of the time
was like the last few minutes, when the
service is over, before one goes out of
church.'

' Well, he must have thought your
silence arose from awe of him, and felt
flattered by it,' suggested Laura. ' He
wants you to take a district.' .

' Take a *what?*' cried Nanny.

' A district,' broke in Adela glibly.
' It's quite easy.   You knock at the door
of the cottages, and the woman who
opens the door looks you up and down

and dusts a chair for you. But if it's a child who comes, it turns its back upon you and shouts " Mo-*thur !*" And you mustn't be frightened, but stand still till " Mo-*thur* " comes.'

'But I shan't know what to do or what to say!'

'What to do is very simple : you have only to sit still and smile. As for what to say, if you see an old woman about, or an old man, you ask after their rheumatism. They're sure to have rheumatism, but they'll be delighted, and think you must have been asking about them to have learnt that. Then you ask the names of the children, and what standards they have passed. When you've been told, you wag your head and look surprised, as if you thought it wonderful for them to have got on so fast. Then you leave a tract, and you come away.'

'Oh, I could never leave tracts !' exclaimed Nanny; 'it seems so impertinent.'

'You don't understand,' said Laura, shaking her head. 'Leaving tracts at cottages is just like leaving cards at your friends' houses : they'd be awfully offended if you forgot. The only difference is that you leave the tract whether they're at home or not. They read just as much of the tract, too, as your friend does of the card—the name. It's a matter of etiquette merely.'

'Dear me ! dear me !' broke in poor Mrs. Bambridge, with a distressed face. 'You will think them very flippant, Captain Ryder ; but I assure you my girls are really very good at parish work, and the Vicar has said over and over again he doesn't know what he should do without them.'

' I don't want to be assured that they do everything they undertake in the very best possible way. They carry their characters in their faces, and their work is done none the less well that they do it with smiles instead of sour looks,' he answered.

The good lady beamed upon him, and proceeded to treasure up that speech from the great man of the neighbourhood, for use among her friends. He then asked her at what time in the evening her son Charlie came home from the City. To the great relief of Nanny, who knew on what subject her husband wished to question the young fellow, Mrs. Bambridge answered that he had gone to

Germany on business for the firm he was with.

'His faculty for learning languages is something quite extraordinary,' added the fond mother. 'He mastered German thoroughly in three weeks.'

And with this astounding statement, uttered in the simplest good faith, Mrs. Bambridge looked at Laura and prepared to take leave.

The girls, meanwhile, had succeeded in persuading young Mrs. Ryder to 'take a district,' and they left feeling very proud of their success.

Nanny entered upon the new duties which she had thus hastily undertaken that very week. Her husband encouraged her to do this, as it would give her an occupation while he himself was busy with an exhaustive study of the state of his affairs. The losses entailed upon him by his mother's singular management of the Brent and Bicton property, and the extensive inroads which her allowance made upon his income, made this a very unsatisfactory work. For the elder Mrs. Ryder's dainty little porcelain hands had been used all her life to grasp and to retain, as a matter of right, such good things as came in her way. And although she now offered most gracefully to do without a brougham, and even to sell her jewellery, her hold over her son had become, through long custom, so secure that he rejected the notion with horror, as if it had been proposed that he should send her to the workhouse or commit some other act as shockingly unfilial.

Meanwhile, Nanny had entered upon

her new duties, which proved much more congenial than she had expected. Brent was not a place where the worst, the most appalling poverty abounded; the most distressing cases of want were to be found in the mushroom growth of small houses which had sprung up on the borderland of Bicton. But this part of the parish was not in Nanny's 'district.' From the technical point of view, she did not make a good 'visitor.' She hurried over her visits to the people she did not like—the whining widow who never thought anybody did enough for her, and the lady whose piety in the morning was only exceeded by her inebriety at night. And she saved up her smiles and brightness for the families she found congenial to her. So that the second Miss Hutchins, who was an ideal 'visitor,' stumping round her district like a clockwork train on circular rails, staying exactly ten minutes at each cottage, except in cases of illness, when the infliction lasted fifteen, felt at last bound to remonstrate.

'You must excuse my taking the liberty of speaking to you, Mrs. Ryder,' she went on, when she had opened her subject. She had met Nanny at the corner of the green, as she herself was squelching along in her goloshes to a mothers' meeting at the schoolroom. 'But I am so much older than you are, and I am sure your intentions are good, and so I venture on a little suggestion. Now, Mrs. Wheeler says that no one has been near her for a fortnight, and as she is in your district——'

'But last time I went she slammed

the door in my face. I couldn't very
well shout good advice at her through
the keyhole, could I ? And I couldn't
even scream out " How are you ?" For
I knew how she was—tipsy.'

The second Miss Hutchins looked
grave.

' My dear young lady, you will never
gain sufficient influence over her to be
any check upon her unfortunate pro-
pensity if you treat the matter in that
way. Remember, the sunshine and the
rain fall equally upon the good and
upon the wicked. You should try to
act upon that precept. Now I treat all
alike. I have a formula for each occasion, and I use it irrespective of persons.'

' And what is your formula for a
closed door ?' asked Nanny, with a
mutinous look.

'I am afraid you are not taking my remarks in the right spirit, Mrs. Ryder. While those people you do like,' she went on, more severely than ever, 'you treat exactly as if they were your own friends. Now, the day before yesterday you were at Mrs. Pegg's for three hours!'

'Yes,' Nanny was obliged to admit humbly, 'so I was. Mrs. Pegg had been offered half a day's washing, and the bigger children were at school, and her old father was in bed with rheumatism. She didn't like to leave the little ones in charge of Bobby, because last time when she did, he tried to put the baby in the copper. So I offered to look after them till school was over.'

'Well, of course it was kind,' conservative Miss Hutchins allowed. ' But it isn't usual, and it might lead to jealousy.'

' It isn't usual to have eight children and only nineteen shillings a week to keep them on—at least, I hope not,' corrected Nanny dubiously. ' And certainly *that* wouldn't lead to jealousy.'

' You are very smart with your tongue, and of course I know I am taking a liberty in speaking to you,' began the elder lady stiffly.

Whereat Nanny broke in gently enough :

' No, no, no; please don't speak like that. Indeed, I know as well as you do that I don't do my visiting properly. And you are one of the pillars of the parish work, and it is very good of you to try to help me to do better. But I can't. It's all new to me, and I feel

shy. You have weight among them,
while I have none. Mrs. Wheeler
wouldn't have dared to shut the door
in your face. I was asked to take this
work, you know, and I do it in the only
way I can. I know very well I can't do
much good. But I hope I don't do
much harm, and I should be sorry to
have to give it up, as part of it I like
very much.'

Indeed, since Nanny could not help
brooding over the gloomy family secrets,
she did feel it a relief to have Mrs.
Pegg's welfare to think about as well as
her own. As long as her husband was
with her, she troubled her head very
little about anything. For she grew
fonder of him every day, more appre-
ciative of his devotion, more sceptical
as to the possibility of his having ever

done anything wrong. But when her husband had gone to town to see his solicitor, and she was left alone in the house with old Mrs. Ryder, whose visit to The Grange was not yet at an end, then Nanny would rejoice that she had something better to do than worry her head about the family skeletons.

Nanny had, indeed, been on her way to Mrs. Pegg's when she was attacked by Miss Hutchins; and when the encounter between her and that lady had ended rather lamely on both sides, she went on her way to the cottage stubbornly, in spite of the lecture on favouritism which she had just received.

Mrs. Pegg was an industrious, kindly creature, the only blame attaching to whom was the fact that she was the mother of eight children. This, how-

ever, had soured the old maid district
visitors against her. She was delighted
to see young Mrs. Ryder, whose lively,
youthful manner and kindness to the
children had already warmed the heart
of the hard-working woman to the
pretty lady from The Grange.

'Come in, do, ma'am, out of the
rain,' she said, with a curtsey. 'You
won't mind the place being a bit untidy-
like. My old father he would come
down to-day, because he said he must
see the Captain's lady, and so I've had
to see to dressing him when I should
have been scrubbing my kitchen. You'll
not mind his chatter, will you, ma'am?
He's not exactly soft, but he just jabbers
on—all about his graveyard mostly, for
he used to be sexton at Bicton till they
pulled down the old church and built a

new one eight years ago—" restoring "
they called it. We don't take much
'count of what he says.'

Nanny saw now where Mrs. Pegg's
own conversational fluency came from.
She followed her hostess into the kitchen,
which was also the general living-room;
for this was one of the old-fashioned
cottages, without the modern bay-win-
dows and parlour.

A white-haired old man, with the
vacant, far-away look of the aged poor
in his eyes, raised himself slowly and
with difficulty in his chair by the fire at
her entrance, and instantly began muttering to himself, with his gaze fixed
upon her face. Nanny started at sight
of him. It was the old man whose
words had alarmed her so much on the
day when she and her husband firs

came to Brent together. She came up
to him, shook him shyly by the hand,
and asked if he was well. He shook his
head slowly from side to side, without once removing his eyes from her
face.

'Ah'm very weel,' he said, with a
slight North-country accent — 'con-
siderin', that is.'

And he continued to stare at the young
lady, still muttering to himself, with a
persistency which made her blush.

'There, Ben,' at last broke in Mrs.
Pegg, whose bump of filial reverence did
not seem to be well developed, 'don't sit
lookin' at the lady as if ye was stuffed.
Sit down, ma'am—do sit down !'

And she brought forward a chair,
which Nanny took, still feeling nervous
and awkward under the steady gaze of

the old man's eyes. At last he gave a
portentous nod and spoke again aloud.

'Ay, ay, it do seem strange, it do,
that I should live to see the second wife
o' the man I buried myself seven-and-
twenty yeer agone come next harvest-
toime.'

'Why, father, what nonsense are you
talking? You're enough to frighten the
lady, with your gaping mouth and your
silly tales.'

She saw that the lady had grown quite
white, and that, although she laughed, it
was with an effort.

'That wasn't Captain Ryder, my hus-
band,' she said, in a quavering voice.
'The one you buried was Lieutenant
Ryder, my husband's father.'

The old man shook his head ob-
stinately.

'Lieutenant Ryder and Captain Ryder's
t' same mon. He never had no son—
only one daughter. You may see her
grave in t' owd churchyard now. She
died o' toyphoy fever, and I buried
her.'

Nanny, listening intently, was shaking
from head to foot.

'But it's that Captain Ryder's son I've
married, Ben,' she said, in a broken
voice.

Ben shook his head again.

'He hadn't a son. They lived here
all their married lives together, him and
Lady Ellen, and I ought to know. And
folks said as how he was not in his right
mind at times, and as how it were on
account o' Lady Ellen bein' a bit flighty
like. A fair lass was Lady Ellen ! And
when the child died, it was supposed he

died too. And there was a funeral, and
Lady Ellen lived at The White House
like a widdy. And presently, when all
the old folks had left Bicton, and t' owd
tale was forgotten, there came a bran-
new Vicar along o' the bran-new houses
and bran - new folk. An' they must
needs have a bran-new church, and
t' owd one was pulled down, an' a sight
o' t' owd stones was destroyed. An' the
big tomb o' Lieutenant Ryder was
moved, and his coffin with it, to make
room for the new vestry. An' the side
of the coffin fell in, or were smashed in
—Ah don't rightly remember which way
it was—an' inside were no body, only
bricks and such-like.'

Mrs. Pegg, who had run out into the
wash-house after one of the children,
heard a scream, and ran back into the

house, to find young Mrs. Ryder standing
up, transfixed with terror.

'Now, what have you been a-
doin' of, frightenin' the lady like
that, you silly old man!' began Mrs.
Pegg.

But Nanny made a gesture to her to
be silent, and, sitting down again, spoke
to him in a quiet tone :

'But, if such a thing had happened,
there would have been a great deal of
talk, a great sensation.'

'Nobody knowed about it but the
Vicar an' me. I was bad with the
rheumatiz, and past work, they said; so
they paid me off, and here I be, and
nobody takes no manner o' notice of
what I say, and——'

'And a good job too!' interrupted his
daughter. 'He's been telling you his

old story of the coffin full o' bricks, I
suppose, ma'am.'

'Isn't it true, then?' asked Nanny
quickly.

But her heart failed her, even as she
put the question.

'It's not easy to tell, ma'am, for that
part of the churchyard where the Ryder
tombs are has been cut off by an iron
paling, for it's not used now, as you may
have noticed, ma'am. But it's not likely
to be true, for where's the sense of
buryin' a coffin without yourself in it,
unless you've done somethink dreadful?
Let alone that there must be servants or
undertaker's men or somebody to find
out the truth, and it's human nature to
talk. And if there had been a great
talk and a stir there'd be some old tales
told in the parish yet, I should think,

though so much of it is new, to be
sure.'

' Ay, that's it. I'm one of the last o'
t' owd ones. And I mind there was some
talk when he died, when he was supposed
to die, that is, mostly about Lady Ellen ;
and folks said she was out of her mind,
or nigh it, and had to have someone allus
about to see she did no harm to herself.'

' And—and what—according to your
story—has become of—Lady Ellen ?'

The old man shook his head again.
That was no part of his story.

' Ah don't know; Ah don't know.'
And then, his narrative having come to
an end, it seemed to dawn upon him for
the first time, as he glanced at his listener's
face, that it might not have been altogether pleasant to hear. ' But them's
owd tales,' he said consolingly; ' you've

no need to take on about them, ma'am.
He's a fine gentleman still, is the Captain,
for all he's grown a bit white about the
head; and if he chose to bury himself
before the time to get rid of a light wife,
why, I don't blame him, seein' he's
known how to get a better.'

Nanny laughed faintly, and rose to
go, speaking a few words to the old
man on indifferent subjects in the hope
of hiding the effect his story had had
upon her. But she looked so white and
woe-begone that Mrs. Pegg followed
her to the door solicitously, with an expression which portended a lecture for
the old man by-and-by.

'Don't scold him,' whispered young
Mrs. Ryder, as she went out.

Then, not forgetting to ask after
those children who were at school, she

bade Mrs. Pegg good-bye, and hurried home.

The strange story she had heard to-day, which, if not absolutely true in all its details, had, she felt sure, a measure of truth in it, disturbed her again, just as, with the elasticity of youth, she had got over the effects of her former discoveries, in the sunshine of her husband's affection.

Although she had the strength of mind to resolve to say nothing to her husband about old Ben's story, she was unable to recover from the effects of it before meeting him, since he had re-turned from town during her absence from home. She found him, too, in a very angry and gloomy mood. He had missed an appointment in town, to begin with; on returning, he had asked his mother for some details concerning some property he had on the Thames, and had received a very unsatisfactory account. Out of ten good-sized cottages which he owned in that neighbourhood, he had, for the last half-year, only received the rents for two. When Nanny came into the study, therefore, she found Dan frowning over the accounts, and his mother sitting at the opposite side of the table, looking white and worried.

'They have been cheating you, mother,' Captain Ryder said, as he rose abruptly upon his wife's entrance. 'It's quite early. I'll run down there to-day and find out what the real facts are. And you, child,' turning to his wife, 'look as pale as a lily. I'll take you with me; it will do you good. It's going to clear up and be fine for the rest of the day.'

Nanny expressed herself delighted to

go, none the less that she saw a look of acute terror pass over her mother-in-law's face. She ran upstairs to change her boots for a cleaner pair, and was not surprised to hear old Mrs. Ryder's knock on the door as she was buttoning them. Metaphorically, Nanny placed herself in fighting attitude as she cried ' Come in.' She guessed what sort of encounter was in store for her.

' Do you want to send your husband mad?' was the old lady's abrupt opening.

' No,' answered Nanny, springing to her feet and crossing to the door, ' neither do I want to go mad myself, mamma. But I have gone near it lately in the maze of mysteries I've been living in. I am hoping that to-day may be the end of some of them.'

' You silly, headstrong girl! Can't

you trust the experience of a woman old enough to be your mother? I tell you there is someone living at Teddington who must be warned before Dan goes there.'

'Warned! Of what?'

'Of—of the change in him which his illness has brought about.'

'What change? I can see none.'

'You! You have no eyes!' cried her mother-in-law contemptuously. 'But there is a change. He is ill; he is not himself. If he should meet——'

Dan's voice broke upon them, calling loudly that if Nanny did not come down at once they would lose the last available train, and have to put off their expedition till next day. A light came into old Mrs. Ryder's face. She turned quickly, and made for the door, with the evident

intention of delaying the journey by
stratagem.   Nanny, however, was wily
enough to guess her intention, and was
outside the door in an instant.

'Good-bye, mamma; I'm sorry I
can't wait now,' she cried, as she flew
down the stairs.

Her husband was standing at the
bottom.   He held out his hands, and
she took them and jumped to the ground
like a child.

'That's right, child.   Why, what is
the matter with you?   You seem all on
fire.'

'It's—hurry,' panted Nanny, as she
dragged him along and out by the front-
door, madly eager to be out of range of
her mother-in-law's wiles.

Her heart beat high with excitement.
If the old lady were right, and if there

should be some tragically interesting encounter in store for them, was it not better than this eternal suspense, this frightful uncertainty whether she was legally Dan's wife or not?

Yet, when once she found herself in the train, with her husband's loving face opposite to her, a panic of terror seized her lest this might be the last hour in which she might hold him truly as her own.

CHAPTER V.

Captain Ryder was very silent and thoughtful during the whole of the journey to Teddington. Almost the only remarks he made on the way were expressions of regret at his own folly in having allowed his mother to have control over his affairs for so long. Nanny did her best to appease his anger against the old lady, believing, as she did, that the latter had probably only retained the management of the property on account of her son's attack of insanity.

'I suppose, Dan dear, she only thought she was saving you trouble,' suggested Nanny timidly.

'I suppose so. And being a lazy man, with a hatred of business, I have only myself to thank for the fact that she has made a hopeless hash of it. Here's a row of ten cottages at Teddington, which we are going to see; eight of them are admitted to be inhabited, and yet I am getting rent from only two of them. And the strangest part of it is that my mother does not err in ignorance. She seems to know exactly what is going on in every corner of the property, and yet to be quite satisfied with a state of things by which three-fourths of my tenants live rent-free at my expense!'

This was a little difficult to explain, certainly. Poor old Mrs. Ryder could

surely not be paying blackmail to as
many as six families in order to guard
the family secrets !

'I don't even know the name of the
man who is supposed to look after the
place,' grumbled Captain Ryder presently. 'Only that he lives at Clairville.
What a name to give to a cottage ! Of
course, he lives rent-free. And equally
of course, it is fair to suppose, the rents
which he collects diminish greatly in
filtering through his hands. Here we
are. Now to explore.'

Captain Ryder had never been to
Teddington before, and did not know
which way to turn until he had asked
for directions. Nobody, however, had
heard of a cottage called Clairville, and
they might have returned to Brent
without having found the place at all

had not Nanny suddenly suggested to
her husband not to ask for it as a
' cottage.'

' Perhaps they would call it a " house "
down here,' she said, rather timidly ; for,
indeed, the idea was born of some mis-
trust of old Mrs. Ryder's truthfulness.

Captain Ryder frowned at this hint,
but he took it, and with instantaneous
success.   For a passing tradesman, on
being asked if he knew a house called
Clairville, assented at once, adding :

' Bob Hanks's place.   Go right down
through the village, and then it's the turning to the left, by the church—a good
way along, facing the river.'

Captain Ryder, after having received
this direction, walked on in silence so
gloomy that Nanny wondered what there
could have been in the man's words to

cause such a change in him. At last he
spoke.

' Robert Hanks,' he said suddenly,
' was the name of a man who was for
many years butler in our family. He
was always writing to my mother while
we were abroad. But she never explained the position he held here. I
can't understand it.'

Poor Nanny shuddered, and wished
her husband would go back without pro-
secuting his inquiries any further. If
this Hanks, an old servant of the family,
was now installed here as caretaker and
rent-collector, with a liberal allowance
as to perquisites, there must be some
strong reason for such generosity ; and
since Dan was evidently ignorant of the
reason, he would do no good, but might
do much harm, if he indulged in any

such expression of his feelings as he apparently meditated. She dared not, however, do more than expostulate very faintly, and her husband paid no heed to her gentle words.

They took the turning by the church, and came presently—not to a row of cottages, but, as Nanny had feared, to a terrace of pretentious 'villa residences,' with bay windows, broad flight of steps, and a ' private road.'

Nanny stopped before the first of these and glanced timidly at her husband. On the glass above the door was the name ' Clairville ' in gilt letters.

' So this is what my mother calls a cottage !' said Dan, as he pulled angrily at the bell.

An old man came to the door in his shirt-sleeves, with a pipe in his mouth

and a child in his arms. There was the
'cut' of a servant about him still, and
Nanny guessed that it was Robert Hanks.
The man seemed startled at sight of
Captain Ryder, whom he saluted with
instant recognition, which did not, however, appear to be mutual.

'Are you Robert Hanks?' asked Captain Ryder.

'Yes, sir. Will you walk in?'

He had taken his pipe out of his
mouth, and he stepped back and stood
aside for the lady and gentleman to pass
into the front room, the door of which
he opened as he spoke.

'I suppose you don't know who I
am,' went on his visitor.

'Oh yes, sir,' answered Hanks readily,
lowering his voice, however, as if there
might be something unwelcome in the

admission ; ' you're Captain Ryder,
sir.'

Although the man's manner was civil,
there was in it that suggestion of latent
insolence which the consciousness of
power over their superiors gives to the
vulgar.

' How did you know that ?' asked
Captain Ryder abruptly.

The man seemed rather reluctant to
go into details.

' I heard from Mrs. Durrant, sir, as
how you were—you were—about, sir.
And I'm very happy to see it, I'm sure,
sir.'

' Perhaps you won't feel quite so
happy when I tell you that I've come to
inquire into the management of these
houses, cottages, or whatever you call
them,' said Captain Ryder, who did not

appear to be favourably impressed by his agent's manner. ' I see there are only two boards up, and yet I am only receiving rents for two. That leaves five houses to be accounted for. Now, how is that ?'

' If you will ask——' Suddenly the man, in whose tone there was a rising note of insolence, glanced at Nanny, stopped, and then framed his answer differently. ' I've given in my accounts in the usual quarter, sir,' he said, ' and no fault has been found with them.'

' Well, but who occupies the other houses ?' asked the puzzled landlord, who began to perceive that there was rather the insolent firmness of conscious right in the man's attitude than the uneasiness of fearful roguery.

'Mrs. Durrant has one, sir, and the rents of two of the others——' began the man.

Captain Ryder echoed his words in astonishment.

'Mrs. Durrant has one and the rents of two of the others! Why, what on earth——'

He stopped suddenly, and after a pause, during which the expression of his face grew more and more angry, while Hanks continued to look demurely at the carpet, he said, in a dry tone :

'And the rents of the remaining two —you take them, I suppose ?'

'Why—er—yes, sir,' answered Hanks, with perfect assurance, still keeping his eyes on the ground as if he feared they might betray a knowledge which would

infer a lack of respect if he raised them
to his landlord's face.

Captain Ryder stood for a few
moments lost in consideration of these
remarkable disclosures.   Then, as if
mechanically, he turned to the door.
Hanks opened it respectfully.

'You are satisfied, I hope, sir, now
that you—that you understand.'

'I don't understand,' interrupted Captain Ryder shortly, as he walked through
the hall towards the front-door.

'Well, sir, there's others that do,' said
Hanks, with the nearest approach to open
impudence that he had shown ; 'and it's
from them, sir, that I look for the wages
I get for my—discretion.'

Captain Ryder, who had reached the
steps, turned quickly.

'I'm afraid you will find,' said he

quietly, as he met the man's eyes with his own, 'that that quality has gone down in the market.'

Nanny followed her husband, with her heart full of dread. What was he going to do next? There was on his face an expression of mingled bewilderment and anger which alarmed her, and made her ask herself in terror whether he was on the brink of another outbreak of the mental malady which had before clouded his life. His lips moved as he walked along with bent head and flashing eyes, and he seemed to be talking to himself and to have forgotten her presence altogether.

'Where are you going, Dan?' she ventured to ask at last.

She had to repeat the question before he stopped short to answer her.

'I'm going to see this woman, this
Mrs. Durrant, to hear what she has to
say for herself.'

But this proposal filled Nanny with
alarm. Dan was angry, Mrs. Durrant
was vindictive : what good could come
of their meeting just now ? This woman
had rendered him important services, she
had cared for him when he was unable
to care for himself.   It was ungenerous,
it was unlike Dan, to haggle over the
payment now.   The mere fact, too, that
he appeared for the moment to have
forgotten these services, and to speak of
Mrs. Durrant as if she had been a
stranger, frightened Nanny. His mother,
Pickering, Valentine Eley — all had
uttered warnings as to the effects his
late illness might leave upon his mind.
Were not these effects already manifest

in this unnatural ingratitude towards the
woman who had tended him in his
illness? Nanny, who was even now a
little jealous of Mrs. Durrant, remembering the meeting she had witnessed in the
grounds of The White House, felt that
there was something suspicious about
this altered attitude towards her. As he
had forgotten to ask Hanks in which
house Mrs. Durrant lived, however,
Nanny was hoping the interview might
even yet be avoided, when, just as they
reached the end of the private road, she
saw the lady who had been caretaker at
The Grange coming towards them. ·

Nanny hung back, feeling a strong
reluctance to be present at the meeting
between her husband and the woman
who was identified with the period of
his insanity. Captain Ryder had turned

round and was looking at the terrace
they had just passed, as if wondering
which was the house he wanted. As he
stood thus, his wife nervously watching
him from the other side of the road,
whither she had hastily retreated, Mrs.
Durrant, who had no companion but a
small fox-terrier, sauntered up. She was
so much occupied in calling to the dog,
which, being little more than a puppy,
had not yet learnt to follow very well,
that she took no notice of either of the
two visitors. Nanny noticed that Dan
continued to stare at the houses, without
appearing to recognise the lady's voice.

It was not until Mrs. Durrant was
close to him that he turned round, being,
indeed, obliged to move then, as he was
standing in the middle of the narrow
footpath. As they thus met face t face,

she uttered an exclamation of amazement, and then, putting her hand on his
sleeve, said in a loud, hearty voice:

' Ralph, my dear old Ralph, what on
earth brings you here ?'

Captain Ryder drew himself up and
stared at her with a frown.

' I have come here to look after my
rents, madam,' he answered simply.

Mrs. Durrant started, withdrew her
hand from his arm, and retreated a
couple of steps, staring at him in her
turn. Then from him her eyes wandered to Nanny, who had come a little
nearer, and was standing in the middle
of the road. So they all stood for a few
seconds, which seemed interminable to
Nanny. Captain Ryder continued to
look with frigid amazement at the lady,
who, on her side, seemed at first to be

struck dumb with dismay. Recovering
herself speedily, however, she burst out
into loud, hysterical laughter, reeled from
the path into the road, and fell down
unconscious.

Captain Ryder looked down at the
figure prostrate in the dust with an
expression of contempt and disgust,
which changed to one of deep annoyance as he glanced at his wife, as the
latter stooped to raise the woman's head.

'Don't touch her, child. I'll call
Hanks. Perhaps he can tell us where
the woman lives.'

Appalled by his callousness, Nanny
glanced up at him, uncertain what to do.

At that moment, however, the door of
one of the houses in the terrace flew
open, and a white-capped maid ran
down the steps towards the group.

'Oh, she's fainted! Oh, what have they done to you, ma'am?' cried the girl.

To Nanny's surprise, she saw, as she looked up, a look of recognition pass between Dan and the servant, who was an exceedingly pretty young girl. It was not a nod or a smile on either side, but it was a quite conclusive sign that they had met before. Indeed, the girl's next words confirmed this impression.

'Oh, sir,' she said indignantly, 'to think of your leaving her to lie in the road like that!'

'Is she your mistress?' he asked, with an appearance of sudden interest.   .

The girl did not answer him. She was busy lifting Mrs. Durrant's head from the ground.

'Come, Nanny; she is all right. We can do nothing more,' said he impatiently

to his wife, as he raised her from her
stooping position over Mrs. Durrant,
who had now opened her eyes.

Nanny felt stupefied with terror at his
strange behaviour. But she obeyed
without a word, and allowed him to
draw her arm through his and lead her
away, as she saw Mrs. Durrant was
rapidly recovering.

' Hadn't we better stay, Dan, until she
can go into her house? I thought—I
thought you wanted to speak to her,'
faltered Nanny.

' So I did, but then I did not expect to
find her in this condition.'

' Condition ! What do you mean by
" this condition," Dan ?'

' Why, that the woman is undoubtedly
tipsy. Didn't you see her seize me, and
hear her call me by my Christian name ?'

'Yes,' whispered Nanny hoarsely.

'Well, could you want any further
proof that she was tipsy? A woman
whom I never saw before in my
life!'

Nanny almost staggered. Was he
trying to deceive her? Or had he
really forgotten? The poor child did
not know which to believe, or which to
hope. There was in his manner, and in
the expression of his face, an absorption
which was quite new to her. He said
little, and she was equally silent, as they
retraced their steps along the road as far
as the church. From time to time,
however, he shot down at her grave,
frightened face a keen, suspicious glance,
under which her eyes fell. At the
corner by the church he stopped.

'You must be tired,' he said shortly.

'We must try to find some place where I can get you a cup of tea. Let me see, the river runs on the left. If we take this road, then, we are sure to find an inn or some place for refreshment on the bank.'

His guess proved a safe one. The road they took led past another terrace of red-brick villas on the one side, and a row of picturesque cottages on the other, straight to the ferry over the river; and close to the water's edge, on the right hand, was a trim garden running up to a snug little riverside inn, where, at this late season of the year, only a couple of local idlers were holding revel.

Captain Ryder and his wife had the coffee-room to themselves.

It seemed to the latter, who, however, took care not to appear to be watchful, that Dan was restless and uneasy. He complained, too, of headache, which Nanny knew to be a bad sign, and although he made no further reference to the events of the afternoon, he evidently brooded over them, and glanced furtively at his wife from time to time, as if wondering what she thought of it all.

When they had had some tea, Nanny, who saw that her husband was very tired, persuaded him to lie down on the little horsehair sofa. He had done too much in one day for a man who had been recently ill, and she was afraid of the combined effects of fatigue and excitement upon him. To her great relief, in a few minutes he fell asleep.

Nanny stole to the window and looked

out. The darkness of night was coming
on. Already the dahlias and chrysanthe-
mums had lost their bright colours, and
the green of the trim lawn and of the
evergreen shrubs had melted into gray.
The October evening breeze shook the
yellowing leaves off the trees until they
sprinkled the grass and lay in little heaps
on the gravel-walks. The river ran, like
a glistening thread of silver-gray, not
fifty feet away from the window, and
the sound of the rushing water at the
weir made an unceasing accompaniment
to the rough voices of the men at the
ferry.

A voice which Nanny recognised
startled her by asking a question of someone who stood near the inn door.

'Has my son been round? I expected him at home before now.'

It was the voice of the old ex-butler, Robert Hanks. Nanny, in desperate excitement, drew back a little. But it was too dark for anyone outside to see her as she stood behind the muslin curtains.

The answer was in the landlord's voice.

'Your son? Yes. He was in the bar just now. Said he was going to have a pipe in the garden before going home. Hi, Thomas!' he went on, raising his voice, ' here's the old man come after you.'

A youngish man in a light suit, who, to judge by his face and bearing, belonged to a far less respectable type than his father, sauntered up from a summer-house at the bottom of the garden. He was smoking a pipe with the air of a man who rarely did anything more laborious. His father, who was evidently still at a high pitch of excitement over the visit of his landlord, seized him by the arm, and, thrusting him into a seat on the lawn, began to pour into the younger man's ear, in a low voice, the history of the visit he had had that afternoon.

The window of the coffee-room was a little way open, and Nanny did not scruple to push it up a little higher, and to listen with all her ears.

At first, however, the old man, mindful of the near neighbourhood of the house, and consequently of possible listeners, kept his voice so low that Nanny could scarcely catch one word. But as his excitement rose, his tones rose also, and at last she could plainly hear

his indignant protests at the treatment he
had received.

'If I'd been just a old servant, and
nothing more, it would be shabby,' was
the first sentence which she could clearly
make out, 'to wish to deny me the
means to pass my old age in comfort.
And them as well able to afford it as the
Ryders too! But when it comes to a
family as I may say I hold in the
holler of my hand!'

'Eh?' ejaculated the young man, half
stupidly, 'the what?'

'The holler of my hand,' repeated his
father doggedly. 'That's what I said,
and that's what I mean. Do you think
the old lady, who was always a near one,
would have let me have the rents of two
of these houses and the use of a third for
all these years for nothing? Not she!'

'No, of course not. I always understood it was for holding your tongue about the old gentleman's goings on when he was off his head.'

'That's not all, not half all. What would that matter at this time of day if that was all?'

'Why, it wouldn't be nice for the family for it to be known that the old gentleman, in a fit of D.T., killed his own child!'

Nanny, listening, with white, parted lips and starting eyes, at the window, scarcely repressed the cry which seemed to tear her breast.

The old man laughed hoarsely.

'Why, that's nothing to what *I* know —that's nothing to what *I'm* paid for keeping quiet!' cried the old man, as his voice became tremulous with excite-

ment. 'And keep it quiet I have, even
from you, my own son; and would have
done till my dying day if they'd only
treated me fair. But now I'm threatened
with being turned out after all these
years, I've done with them! And I
don't care who knows what I know,
and that is that the gentleman who
murdered his little daughter Ellen in
the corner room at Brent Grange
never died at all, though he is supposed to be buried in Bicton Churchyard!'

Nanny felt her knees give way under
her. She clung to the window-sill,
leaning her wet face on her hands. The
darkness had set in rapidly during the
last few minutes; the colours of the
garden had all sunk to gray and black;
and the river, with the last rays of day-

light upon it, shone more brightly in the
dusk.

The younger man was startled also.

'Come, I say, guv'nor, ain't that
pitching it rather strong?'

'It's as true as I'm sitting here,'
returned the old man, slapping his knee.
'They managed it, Lady Ellen and her
people, very careful and clever, and even
the undertaker's men didn't know but
what there was a man in the coffin. But
somebody always finds out these things,
and that somebody was me. They paid
me off handsome, and handsomely I've
kept their secret till to-day, when in
walks the very man who was supposed
to be put underground, and says, says he,
" Discretion's gone down in the market,"
says he. And with that he threatens, or
as good as threatens, to turn me out.'

There was a pause, during which the elder man slapped his knee again, and the younger ejaculated from time to time, ' Well, I'm blest !' and similar sympathetic observations. He was a practical young man, however, and not needlessly vindictive.

' Well, but what good will it do you to round on 'em now ?' he asked presently. ' Nobody would believe you after all this time. You can't do rich folks like that no harm, unless you're richer than them.'

The old man shook his head knowingly.

' There's somebody else will do that for 'em,' he said dryly. ' That Mrs. Durrant—she's a party that can keep a thing close, too—she's been treated just the same way. And she's simply

packed up her things and gone off, with
a look in her eye that bodes no good to
somebody. She didn't not to say exactly
confide in me, but she just said that if
the Ryders had treated me rough, I
needn't fret ; for she was just going to
set about such a revenge on 'em as they'd
never forget. Ay, and she looked as if
she meant it, too !'

Nanny shivered. Every word these
men uttered was like a fresh blow.

' I might be sorry for him, knowing
the life her ladyship used to lead him,
and how it was that that drove him to
drink, if he hadn't had the impudence to
bring with him this afternoon a little lass
as pretty as a picture, and calls himself
her husband, I'll be bound ! And me
knowing her ladyship's alive all the
time ! I say it's a shame, and it'll serve

him right if Mrs. D. do make him suffer.'

Nanny fell back half fainting, and lay for a few minutes in a heap on the floor, with her head against a chair.

Then Dan's voice startled her, almost drawing a cry from her dry lips.

' Nanny, Nanny, my darling, where are you ?'

CHAPTER VI.

AT the sound of her husband's voice Nanny dragged herself to her feet and tottered unsteadily across the room towards him.

There was no light in the room, the service, in these off-season times, being of a very perfunctory kind.

'Are you ill, Nanny? What is the matter? Why don't you answer me?'

His tone was pettish and irritable.

'No, I am quite well, dear,' she

answered, trying hard to steady her voice, but not entirely succeeding.

A murderer! The murderer of his own child! She did not want the light to come, dreading, as she did, to look again upon his face. But yet she must make some excuse to keep away for a few minutes from the touch of his hands. So she crossed the room to the fireplace, and pretended to fumble for the bell-handle.

'You have been asleep, dear, I think,' she said; 'and I did not want them to wake you by bringing the light in. But I think we really must have some illumination now.'

He muttered an assent, and, raising himself slowly from the sofa, went towards the window.

'Why, I do believe there is that rascal

Hanks!' he exclaimed, peering out into
the dusk. 'I have a great mind to go
out to him and——'

Before he could utter another word,
Nanny had flown across the room to
him, and was hanging on his arm. The
thought that he might, by further rousing the anger of the ex-butler, be
running ignorantly into danger, brought
back in a moment enough of her old
feelings of affection and loyalty to make
her eager to protect him. Looking out,
she saw that Hanks and his son had left
the seat near the window, and had
strolled down as far as the water's edge.
She pulled down the sash, saying as she
did so :

'I shouldn't trouble myself any more
about the fellow, Dan. Or, if you must
take any further steps in this matter of

the rent, why, I am sure it would be better to put it in your lawyer's hands.'

She ended this speech in a low voice, for the girl who now filled the places of waiter, barmaid, and chambermaid had come in with candles. Nanny herself pulled down the blind; she did not want Hanks to see her husband again.

Dan looked at her in astonishment. It was quite a new *rôle* for his girl-wife, that which she was now playing—of adviser. And that half-tremulous assurance of manner with which she was moving about, surely that was something new also. To the newly-married husband, however, every change of mood in his young wife was adorable, and, as soon as the girl had left the room, Dan followed Nanny to the glass, before

which she was putting on her hat. She
blushed with fear. He would see the
change in her face, she was sure. She
herself saw it, and knew that the horrible definite knowledge learned in the
past half-hour had made her older, years
older.

But Dan saw only the charm of a
fresh mood, and he came behind her,
and clasped her in his arms, and laughed
at her for her sermons. Nanny's eyes
filled suddenly with tears as they met his,
and he asked her, with tender solicitude,
what was the matter.

' Nothing, nothing, nothing,' she answered, laughing almost hysterically.
' It was only a silly thought that came
into my head.'

' Well, and what was the thought?
Of course it was silly, coming through

that little head ; it acquired the head's own quality. But what was it ?'

Nanny hesitated, and hid her head on his shoulder, trembling convulsively.

' I was only thinking—that one must always like people—for what they are to one's self. That is all one must trouble about. So you like me,' she went on in jerks, with her head still buried, 'because of what I am to you ; and you don't like me any the less because I was a rather tiresome and disobedient daughter. And so I—like you——'

Her voice broke, and Dan finished the sentence for her in a grave and rather preoccupied tone :

' So you like me, little one, even if you think it is a shame that I should turn out a lot of lazy ruffians who have been allowed for years to draw a com-

fortable income for doing nothing whatever.'

'But, Dan dear, your mother must
have known what she was about. I
don't think she is particularly open-
handed, and if she paid these people
highly, I expect it was " for value
received." '

It was a difficult suggestion to make,
for Nanny could not tell with what half-
memories he might be struggling. His
face clouded, indeed, and with frowns he
seemed to be trying to recall some lost
impression. However, he only said
abruptly :

' Of course. We must get back home,
and wrestle with her constitutional
inability to tell more than one-sixteenth
of the truth.'

And he seemed on the instant to burn

with impatience to be home, rang the
bell, paid the bill, and hurried Nanny up
through the village to catch the next
train.

They were only at the station just in
time. But Nanny saw, as they ran
along the platform and dashed headlong
into the nearest compartment, the face of
Mrs. Durrant at the window of the next
carriage but one.

They came face to face with her at
Bicton Station, where she secured the
only fly, and loudly gave the direction
to The White House. Captain Ryder
heard this, and looked at her with an
expression of strong disapprobation, but
he made no remark. Indeed, his manner
puzzled his wife greatly. She saw that
he was both perplexed and annoyed.
From time to time he would put his

head in his hands, and remain for some
minutes without uttering a word. Then
presently he would start up and smile at
her, or address to her some remark full
of playful affection, but without the
slightest allusion to the matters which
were evidently troubling him. The
poor child, with her heart bleeding with
pity for him, could only wait and
watch.

On arriving at Brent Grange they
were met by a piece of news which
surprised neither of them. Old Mrs.
Ryder had left for town. She had
written a pretty little note to her
daughter-in-law, and put it on the
latter's writing - table. Having just
heard, the note said, of the illness of a
dear old friend, the writer felt bound to
return to Kensington for a few days, but

she hoped that, now Dan was well
again, they would not mind. She would
be back again in a week, or before then
if they wanted her; and she remained,
with a thousand kisses, her dear Nanny's
affectionate mother.

Dan read the missive through without
a word. Nanny wished he would not
be so silent. This taciturnity seemed to
her ominous. She dressed for dinner,
which had been kept back for them till
nine o'clock, in her prettiest frock; she
exerted herself to be lively and sweet to
him. But during the progress of the
meal a heavy gloom seemed to settle
upon him, before which her efforts
grew faint and weak, until at last, when
dessert had been placed on the table,
and they were left alone together in
the big room, they sat on in a dead

silence, and there was no sound in the room but the soft little splash of a rose-water table-fountain, one of Nanny's few wedding presents, and formerly the delight of her heart.

'Shall we go, dear?' she said at last.

For the candles, with their pretty little silk shades, the sparkling glass, the great silver shells piled with fruit, had begun to swim in a mist of tears before her eyes. There was a wicked spirit haunting her husband, the young wife felt, which might rise and seize him at any moment from out of those remote dark corners where sombre family portraits kept guard over ancient presses and chests.

Dan looked up with a start, and Nanny, trembling, repeated her words.

'Oh, yes, yes, we will go,' said he absently.

And he held open the door for her, and followed her out. But before she could turn to take his arm, as she meant to do, to take him to the drawing-room, where she meant to try the effect on him of such musical accomplishments as she possessed, he had slipped away quietly to his study, and she was left alone.

The study! Nanny did not like his going into the study, which, from the frights both she and her husband had suffered there, had acquired in her eyes the character of a haunted room. He had not been in there since his accident, and it was with a superstitious feeling that there was something unlucky, uncanny, about the apartment, which

boded ill to her husband, that Nanny,
after a little hesitation, went slowly
across the hall towards the passage
which led to the study. Even the rustle
of her frock, a light gray silk, Nanny's
very best, frightened her, and made her
hurry faster along the polished floor.

But when she got to the study-door,
she felt too timid to knock at it. After
all, what excuse could she give? It
was the very essence of the poor young
wife's trouble that she dared not confess
to her husband what it was that distressed
her—dared not even hint to him that
she knew his secret, and shared his
evident fear lest his madness should
return.

She heard him throw open one of the
windows—heard him unlock his cigar-
cabinet, and presently strike a light.

Should she go in now and try to persuade him to smoke in the drawing-room, as his mother had always forbidden him to do? Or, at least, should she ask that she might stay with him in the study, pleading that she felt lonely? As she asked herself these questions, and brought her little knuckles, ready for the knock, nearer and nearer to the door, she heard a sudden and loud noise inside the room.

A chair had fallen with a crash into the fireplace, and Dan had uttered a loud cry and an oath.

Then : 'Who are you? What' are you? It's gone—gone!' she heard him say in a husky whisper.

The next moment she was in the room.

Dan was leaning back against the wall

by the window, with his head bent on his
breast, and wild eyes. A couple of candles
were on the table, flickering in the
draught. There was no one else in the
room, no one in the darkness outside.
Nanny shut the door, came timidly up
to him, and tried to put her white arm,
which was bare to the elbow and shining
with diamonds he had given her, through
his.

He looked up at her with a heavy,
gloomy face, and shrank away, repulsing
her, but very gently.

' Go away, child!' said he hoarsely.
' I—I have seen—seen—something. I
—I am afraid, Nanny, my darling,
darling wife, I have done you an awful,
unspeakable wrong!'

In a paroxysm of anguish, the man
thrust his head into his hands, sobbing

aloud, pressing his fingers, his nails, into his flesh as if he would tear it from the bones. Nanny shook from head to foot, but it was with no selfish distress, but with pain for him, with sympathy for him, the man she loved, in his fearful distress.

'Don't push me away! Oh, let me come near you—let me comfort you, Dan! I am your wife—your own loving wife!' she cried imploringly. 'What you say doesn't matter. What you have done doesn't matter. Nothing in the world matters to me but this —that I love you, that I am your wife!'

But he hardly seemed to hear her. As she pressed herself against him, trying to twine her arms about his neck, he suddenly looked up, and, seizing her

arms in his hands, held her away from
him and looked into her eyes.

'I—I have delusions,' he said, in a low
voice.

But to Nanny this was no fresh blow.
It was with only a more tender note
of pity in her voice that she said :

'Have you, Dan? Then let me comfort you. See, Dan, my love is no delusion. While I am with you it will be all
right. You will see nothing but my face.'

But he drew back, and, looking into
her eyes with plaintive intentness, said :

'Nanny, you have seen this coming
upon me! Tell me, you have, have you
not?' Then, as she did not answer, but
lowered her eyes, he sighed, and went
on : 'There is no need for you to answer
me. I have seen it in your face.'

After a few moments of silence, during

which she tried, by gentle caresses which
he scarcely seemed to notice, to impress
him with a comforting feeling of her
watchful love, she spoke again, in a very
low, tender voice :

'I think you are not well yet, Dan,
and that is why you fancy strange things,'
she said. 'I think you ought to see a
doctor—not Dr. Haynes, but someone
who has known you longer, who attended
you when——'

She stopped, unable to utter the
terrible words in her mind. Dan
seemed to be roused into a little more
life and energy by the suggestion.   ·

'There is someone I ought to see,' he
said—'someone who will understand
this ; at least, I think so.   I will see her
to-morrow.'

Nanny's face clouded.   She could not

doubt that he alluded to Mrs. Durrant,
whom he had that very afternoon
treated with so little ceremony. What
treatment could he now expect at the
hands of this woman, whose vindictive
expression of face, as they met at the
station, had impressed Nanny so strongly?

Dan went on, after a short pause, as if
thinking aloud:

'And then I will go straight on to
Durham, and find out how things are
being managed there: whether, for in-
stance, there are any more old pensioners
eating up the rents, by my mother's
special favour.'

'Perhaps the change will do you
good, Dan, if you don't worry yourself
too much about things you find going
wrong. When shall we start?' asked
Nanny.

Captain Ryder looked down at her inquiringly ; then laughed and patted her on the shoulder.

'*We* start !' echoed he. 'I am not going to take you, child. I have taken you on one of these inquiry expeditions, you see,' he went on in a coaxing tone, as he noticed the sudden change on her face to blank disappointment, anxiety, and even suspicion, 'and I find it does not answer. I can't relieve my feelings by bad language when you are present, you know, little one.'

'You could leave me at the hotel when you wanted to scold the people,' suggested she. 'Wouldn't you miss me, Dan ?' she went on imploringly. 'Are you so anxious to go away from me already ?'

Dan looked down at her tenderly.

'I shall miss you, Nanny, every hour that I am away. But—I must go alone.'

She attempted no more persuasion. Her arms fell away from his neck, as a torrent of passionate suspicion overwhelmed every other feeling in her heart. If she had not had so much foundation for her doubts of his straightforwardness, his firmness in this matter would have appeared only consistent with his usual adoring but autocratic attitude towards her. But his flat denial that he had ever seen Mrs. Durrant before that afternoon, and his evident recognition of her servant, had prejudiced in Nanny's mind every statement he might make. She was too miserable, too heart-sick, and withal too much afraid of what the consequences might be, to make any open accusation against him; but she drew herself away from him and sat down on a chair by the book-case, with a look on her face which ought to have been eloquent enough for a newly-married man to read.

Captain Ryder, however, seemed blind to looks and deaf to tones. With his eyes for the most part fixed straight in front of him, as if the delusion of which he had spoken was again upon him, he mentioned mechanically some details of his proposed journey: the time at which he would start next day, the number of hours he would be in the train, which showed her that he .had arranged this expedition beforehand.

And this again woke suspicions in Nanny which he could not lull to rest.

What was the ' delusion ' of which he had spoken ? She asked herself this question a dozen times that night as, uneasy and wakeful, she lived through again, in many distorted shapes, the events of the day. Had he really seen Lady Ellen again, as he had seen her on the occasion of his accident? And had she really been married to him? Nanny felt comparatively little uneasiness on this last score. If Lady Ellen were Dan's wife, would she content herself with these stealthy, abortive visits to The Grange, and allow a younger woman to fill her rightful place without one open protest? It seemed to Nanny that this idea was absurd. On the other hand, why should the sight of her—if, indeed, he had seen her—fill Dan with so much horror?

After a restless night, both Captain Ryder and Nanny, heavy-eyed and unrefreshed, sat like spectres over an almost untasted breakfast. Both were disturbed and unhappy, though neither made further confession to the other. Both felt a sensation of relief, mingled with the pain of their first parting, as they bade each other good-bye at Bicton Station.

' You'll write to me, won't you?' said Nanny, as she looked up wistfully, and yet with trouble in her eyes, to her husband, as he stood at the window of the railway-carriage. ' Because I shan't know where to write to myself till you do. But perhaps you don't want my letters—perhaps you would rather not be bothered,' she added, with a touch of half-plaintive coquetry, as he did not at once answer.

' Well, you know,' said he at last, ' I

shan't be gone long, and I may be moving about.'

A shade crossed the young wife's face. He did not want her to write to Durham! Why? Suspicion, jealousy supplied the answer.

As the train moved out of the station, an idea—a miserable, tormenting idea— returned to her. He had let out, perhaps accidentally, the fact that it was a woman whom he intended to consult about his 'delusions.' Nanny had at once jumped to the conclusion that this woman was Mrs. Durrant. Where and when, then, was he going to meet her? Or was it by letter only that this consultation was going to take place?

Nanny pondered these things as she was being driven back to The Grange in her little brougham. On the way she saw the object of her speculations, Mrs. Durrant, with a small bag in her hand, evidently on a shopping expedition. She stopped the carriage and jumped out.

' Oh, Mrs. Durrant,' she cried humbly, ' may I speak to you for one minute ?'

She did not know what she was going to say, and she stood before the other woman, feeling miserably awkward and uncomfortable, remembering that most unsatisfactory meeting of the previous day. Mrs. Durrant looked at her with a bold and supercilious stare, compressing her lips meanwhile with an expression of undisguised malice.

' I am quite at your service, Mrs. Ryder, for as long as you please,' she said, with elaborate mock-courtesy.

Poor Nanny did not know what to say.

'I am so sorry,' she began, 'for what happened yesterday. And I can't understand it at all. The only explanation I can think of is that my husband didn't want me to know that he had ever been —been—ill in his mind,' mumbled the poor young wife, trying in vain to find a more euphemistic phrase, 'and so he pretended not to know you. Of course, I know very well that he did know you, and—and that he is not really ungrateful to you. You do understand, and—and you won't blame him, will you?'

During this speech Mrs. Durrant's face had grown impenetrably cold. Nanny's heart sank as she looked at her.

'You do me more than justice, Mrs. Ryder,' she said. 'What gratitude the

Ryders have to show me will be for favours to come.'

It was only the threat of an angry woman, but it was uttered in such a white-heat of revengeful feeling that it struck terror into Nanny. She was so much afraid, however, of any harm which this woman might do to Dan, and so anxious for an explanation about the mysterious Lady Ellen, that she persevered in attempting to soften her.

'Indeed,' she began again gently, 'you would find it very easy to earn mine if you liked to try. There are things which puzzle me dreadfully, and about which I can't ask my husband, which I should be so very grateful to have explained to me.'

Mrs. Durrant's mouth relaxed a little.

From curiosity or some other cause, her
attitude became more conciliatory.

' Things explained !' she said. ' What
things ?'

' About—about Lady Ellen, for one
thing,' answered Nanny simply. ' Who
is she ? Where does she live ? Why
does she haunt the place, without ever
openly coming forward ? Twice she has
alarmed my husband by appearing to
him——'

Mrs. Durrant became, on the instant,
all closest attention.

' At least,' corrected Nanny cautiously,
' I think it must have been she. Who
else could it have been to alarm him ?
And why did it alarm him ? These
questions puzzle me all night and all
day.'

And Nanny put her hands up to her

head. A minute after, as there came no
answer, she suddenly looked up, and
caught on Mrs. Durrant's face an
eloquent, unmistakable look of mingled
amusement, delight, and malice. The
young wife grew hot and cold. What
had she done ? What secret had she
betrayed ? Her companion seemed to
recollect herself, and answered demurely :

‘ I should be very happy to afford you
the information you require if it were in
my power, Mrs. Ryder. Unfortunately,
I have never even heard of Lady Ellen
Ryder, and therefore I cannot tell you
why her appearance, or her supposed
appearance, alarms your husband. Good-
morning.'

‘ Good-morning,’ said Nanny, trembling, as she got into the brougham.

What had she done ? Had she played

into the hands of this woman, and betrayed to her something she had better have kept to herself?

Nanny passed a day and a night of torment. She received a telegram from her husband, sent from an hotel in Durham, and so far her suspicions were set at rest. He had gone up there as he had arranged.

But as the second day wore on she again grew suspicious and uneasy. Why did he not write?

By the evening post, however, she got a letter. Affectionate, but short and unsatisfactory, it roused again all her vague fears.

'Don't expect another letter from me for a few days,' so ran the latter part of the note; 'an old friend has offered to take me on a cruise, and I may not have

a chance of posting to you for some
days.'

'For some days!' For some days!
Where was he going for those some
days? Suspicion grew in the young
wife's breast until, taking definite form
at last, it took shape in this thought:
Supposing that, feeling his malady
returning upon him, he was going to
put himself again under supervision, as
he had done before, and made the yachting cruise an excuse for not writing to
her!

Nanny flew across the long drawing-
room, where she was sitting alone at her
work, as this thought darted into her
mind. The White House! The White
House! That was where he must have
been shut up. Mrs. Durrant's return
thither had probably been planned by

her husband himself. This last idea maddened her, but it could not be stifled.

She must go there at once; she must find out whether her husband was deceiving her, whether this horrible curse had indeed descended upon him again.

Quickly, silently, she crept up the stairs of the big and now lonely house, put on a cloak and bonnet, and ran out into the grounds by a side-door. Like a hare, she fled in the dusk through the avenues of yellowing trees and along the lonely roads towards The White House.

When she reached it dusk had fallen; the great mansion, still looking more than half deserted, seemed to glare at her in the faint light. There was a lamp in

one of the rooms, and Nanny saw
between the curtains the figures of Mrs.
Durrant and her brother. She crept
close to the barred iron gates, and looked
through into the tangle of shrubs in the
garden. Something — someone was
moving there—creeping slowly through
the bushes. Nanny kept quite still, and
held her breath. The figure came
nearer. It was a man's. Was it
Pickering ?

No, no, no! This word seemed to
ring through her brain like the din of a
hammer. The man came nearer; she
remained quite still. He passed close' to
where she stood, and Nanny had the
self-command not to cry aloud. But it
was partly because she felt stunned.

For the face that looked out, with
haggard, restless, mad eyes, through the

bars in the fading light, was that of Ralph Ryder.

'Dan! My husband!'

The words were formed by her lips, but not sounded. Slowly he went on, forcing his way painfully through the tangled shrubbery, while the heart-broken woman clung to the bars with a face as wild and haggard as his own.

CHAPTER VII.

THE road was deserted. There was no near sound but the crackling and rustling of the shrubs as the unhappy maniac slunk away from the gate, to the bars of which Nanny was clinging. The great white house was growing gray as the twilight faded rapidly into night. The figures of Mrs. Durrant and her brother Valentine were more plainly visible than ever through the curtains of the room on the first-floor in which they were sitting.

Nanny at length found voice enough for a hoarse cry :

' Dan !'

There was no answer, but the rustling
and crackling amongst the shrubs ceased.

' Dan !' she repeated. ' Oh, Dan,
answer me ! Come, let me speak to
you for one moment, only one moment,
Dan !'

The noise among the boughs and the
dead leaves began again, and the stealthy
steps returned. Peering through the
bars into the deep black shadow under
the wall, Nanny saw the figure of Ralph
Ryder among the brushwood, saw the
gleam of the wild eye intently watching
her.

' Oh, my husband ! come nearer,
nearer ! I am not afraid of you, dear.
Nothing in the world could make me
afraid of you. Why didn't you trust
me, Dan, your own wife ? I would

nurse you and care for you better than these creatures could ever do. Come near me, dear.'

She thrust her hand through the bars of the gate towards him. He seemed touched by her appeal, and he moved a step nearer. But suddenly stopping short, when almost close enough to the bars for her to touch him, he uttered a groan, and, turning sharply, disappeared from her sight among the evergreens in the opposite direction.

Nanny could not go away without more satisfaction than this. She ran under the wall to the gate habitually used, and rang the bell. She would see this Mrs. Durrant again, and insist on a proper interview with her husband. She felt that if she could only sit by his side, and take his hands in hers, and look

with her own tender, loving eyes into
his poor stricken ones, her affection
would be able to break down the barrier
his malady had raised between them, and
he would spare her and himself at least
this last most bitter pang of estrange-
ment.   What, after all, could this
boasted care and watchfulness of Mrs.
Durrant's be worth, when she let him
roam about the grounds alone so late at
night ?

Nanny suddenly asked herself whether
Mrs. Durrant and her brother even
knew of the patient's return.   Supposing, as she now could not but do,
that not only the yachting expedition,
but the visit to Durham, were a mere
blind, Dan, feeling that his malady was
returning upon him, must have returned
almost as soon as he had written the

letter warning her not to expect to hear
from him.   Perhaps he had only just
arrived, and, obtaining an entrance with
a private key, had shut himself into the
grounds without having yet shown himself to anybody.

Nanny waited a long time before her
ring brought anybody to the gate.   When
at last rapid steps were heard coming
along the narrow path between the
bushes, they proved to be those of Mrs.
Durrant's pretty maid, the same girl
whose recognition of her husband she
had noticed.   She unlocked the gate
quickly, but uttered a cry on recognising
the visitor.

Nanny took advantage of the maid's
evident surprise and consternation to put
a remark to her abruptly, before she had
time to consider what she ought to say.

'Captain Ryder is here!' she exclaimed decisively.

Even with the evidence of her own
senses to confirm this fact, the acquiescence of the servant gave the poor young
wife a fresh shock.

'Yes, ma'am, he is here.' Then,
perceiving by the lady's involuntary start
what she had done, she tried clumsily to
retract. 'Oh, I mean—at least——'

But Nanny interrupted her impatiently :

'Captain Ryder is here, you say,
walking about these grounds.'

The girl drew a long breath, and
threw a hasty glance back over her
shoulder. In a whisper she answered:

'Ye—es, ma'am.'

'You—you are afraid of him?'

'No—o. At least, I shouldn't be if

Pickering was here. I was hoping
it was Pickering when I came to the
gate. Pickering can manage him when
he has his fits on better than anybody,
better even than Mrs. Durrant.'

'Where has Pickering gone to, then?'

'To see Lady Ellen, I expect,
ma'am.'

'Lady Ellen!'

The servant saw directly, by the
visitor's excitement, that she had said
too much. She tried to close the gate.

'There! Oh dear, I thought you
knew. You did speak as if you knew.
Now I shall get into trouble. Oh,
do go, ma'am, and don't say how I
told you anything. And I didn't,
indeed.'

'No, but I want you to tell me something,' said Nanny very quietly, taking

care to stand within the gate. 'I won't
get you into trouble. I promise. But
I want to see Captain Ryder, my
husband. You must let me come
inside.'

'Oh no, ma'am. Indeed I couldn't.'

But Nanny had settled that question
by springing suddenly well within the
gate. The servant was going to scream,
but Nanny stopped her.

'What is the good of calling out
now?' she said. 'You would only get
scolded for letting me in. But if you
go quietly back to the house it won't
matter to you even if I am seen. For
there are other gates to the grounds, and
it will be taken for granted I got in by
one of them.'

Almost sobbing, the girl let herself be
persuaded, and relocked the gate.

'And now only tell me,' said Nanny,
turning to her again, 'which room does
Captain Ryder sleep in ?'

'I don't know which one he is going
to use this time,' answered the girl
sullenly. 'He's only just come back to
the house.'

'But which one did he use before ?'

'The back ground-floor room in the
left wing.'

Nanny remembered the barely-fur-
nished apartment into which she had
peeped on the occasion of her former
visit to The White House. She was
making her way without further remark
towards the open back-door of the
house, through which she thought she
would slip in quietly, and secreting
herself in her husband's apartment, wait
for his return to it. But she heard the

servant running after her, and then she
felt the girl's hands seizing her cloak.

'No, no, no, you mustn't go in!
Look here, ma'am, I'll tell you something, if only you'll be reasonable and go
away. Mrs. Durrant is rather—well,
rather *excited* herself to-night, and I
wouldn't go in if I was you. And she's
been saying the most awful things about
you, and how she meant to give you
such a fright as you never had in your
life before. And if you was to go in
now, and she was to see you, and all
that lot of wine and spirits about, as
she's been going backwards and forwards
to all the evening——'

Nanny cut her short, saying very
sharply:

'Wine! spirits! Not where Captain
Ryder——'

She stopped. But the girl guessed her thought, and replied to it.

' I'm sure I hope not, ma'am. For last time when he was bad he got hold of just a glass or two of wine, and it made him that wild I declare we all thought he was going to murder us. And so he would, I believe, if Mr. Valentine and Pickering hadn't stopped him, and pushed him into his room and locked him up in it. But now Pickering's away I'm sure I do hope Mrs. Durrant will be careful.'

Her words only encouraged Nanny in the course upon which she had decided. It was plain that Captain Ryder, in his helpless state, had fallen into bad hands, and that at all risks she must do something to protect him against both himself and his so-called guardians. As

the servant still clung to her cloak,
therefore, and paid no attention to either
her pleadings or her protests, Nanny
quickly unfastened the clasp of her
mantle, and leaving that garment in the
girl's hands, dashed through the open
back-door into the house.

She found herself, of course, in the
servants' quarters, but they were deserted,
the establishment kept up by Mr. Valentine Eley in the absence of his sister
being apparently of that modest kind
which depends on outside labour.
Nanny ran hither and thither through
kitchens and passages until she lighted
upon the way to the great hall. This
was sufficiently illuminated for her to
have no difficulty in finding the door of
that back-room which the servant had
indicated as Captain Ryder's.

The door was ajar. Nanny, with a
loudly-beating heart, pushed it open a
few inches further. No one was in it,
but it was clear that an occupant was
expected, for a floating wick burned in a
little glass suspended by a chain from
the ceiling. She noticed now, too, that
iron bars had been placed before each of
the windows. Having given the maid-
servant the slip, Nanny thought she had
better find some hiding-place in which
she could secrete herself until her
husband either came or was brought in.
There was not much choice. The only
possible place of concealment was the
large wardrobe which stood against the
wall nearly opposite the door.

Nanny opened it, found one long
compartment nearly empty, and at once
took her place in it.

Then the minutes seemed to drag on
like hours. She almost thought it must
be drawing towards morning, and that
no one was going to use the room after
all, when sounds of voices and of the
slamming of a door on the floor above
made her push open the wardrobe door
further to listen. Mrs. Durrant and her
brother were disputing: he protesting,
she insisting on some course of conduct
which he disapproved. Still talking
loudly and angrily, they came down the
stairs, and Nanny heard Valentine say:

'Do you know what you're doing,
you madwoman? Don't you know that
to give this man drink is like putting a
match to a petroleum-store? You'll
have him raving before morning if you
do. And then whom do you injure?
The poor devil himself, perhaps, but

much more likely ourselves. For he'll do some mischief, and it will be found out, as sure as fate, who put him in the way of it. Now, be reasonable, there's a good soul!'

All the time brother and sister were evidently drawing nearer to the room where Nanny was in hiding. Mrs. Durrant interrupted her brother occasionally by ejaculatory remarks, but for the most part she only kept up a running accompaniment of malicious and derisive laughter.

'Poor fellow!' she said at last in a mocking tone. 'Why should he be deprived of all the pleasures of life, while others get more than their share? And if he does get a little excited, and give some of the good people at The Grange a fright, I'm sure I shan't blame him.

So you please leave me alone. I know what I'm doing, and I will undertake that we shall come to no harm through my diversion. So now go to bed like a good boy, and mind your own business.'

She spoke so sharply at last that her brother seemed to leave off attempting to dissuade her from her wicked project.

'I shall fasten the case up, then,' said he sullenly. 'If he gets at that we shall have the house set on fire, or something.'

' Not a bit of it,' she answered lightly. 'If he breaks out, it will be straight for The Grange he will go after his wife. However, you can do as you like about that.'

She burst open the door of the room where Nanny was hiding, put something down on the table, still laughing maliciously to herself, and went out again. Valentine Eley was vigorously using a hammer in the hall. There was a little more wrangling discussion between them, and then both went upstairs again.

Nanny came out of her hiding-place, and looked to see what Mrs. Durrant had brought. On the table she found a spirit-decanter containing whisky, and a glass. She at once opened one of the windows, emptied the whisky over the tangled flower-border outside, and carried the decanter out of the room. In the hall she saw the case of whisky which Valentine had fastened up. It was standing away from the wall, where nobody who entered the hall could fail at once to catch sight of it. After a moment's hesitation Nanny determined to try to

move it, to place it somewhere where
her husband, on coming towards his
room, should not be able to see it. It
was an unpleasant thing to do, to wander
secretly about another person's house and
move about things which did not belong
to one; but Nanny felt that her husband's
safety, perhaps his life, was concerned,
and, after all, The White House was
only lent to these people in return for
their proper guardianship of Captain
Ryder. So she put the decanter down on
the hall table, and began to push the case
towards the furthest corner of the hall.

While she was thus engaged she heard
sounds overhead, and before she had
finished her task Mrs. Durrant's voice
called to her from the top of the staircase. ·

'If you please, Mrs. Ryder, may I learn to what fortunate circumstance I am indebted for the honour of this visit? And you might let me know, at the same time, if there is anything else in my brother's house which you would like to have moved.'

Nanny came to the foot of the staircase and looked up. Mrs. Durrant was not intoxicated, but, on the other hand, she was certainly excited, and a little harder of manner and more reckless of speech than usual.

'I must apologize for what I have done,' said Nanny, in a voice that was unsteady in spite of all her efforts; 'I wanted to see my husband, and I was afraid you might not like to let me see him. So I got in like a—a burglar, without asking. But I only want to see him, indeed, and, if you will only let me, I shall be quite satisfied.'

'And what are you doing with that case, may I ask ?'

Nanny hesitated. Surely the woman, who was not, she thought, altogether without feeling, would soften if she pleaded to her.

'I—I was afraid,' she said. 'I wanted to put it out of the way—where he could not see it.'

'And don't you think it is taking a good deal upon yourself to move about other people's property?'

'Oh, don't be so hard! You know why I did it. It was for my husband's sake. Can't you understand how I feel for my own husband?'

'I don't know anything about your husband, I'm sure; nor why you should

think he must be so anxious to tamper
with other people's property.'

'Sh!' whispered Nanny. 'He is
coming!'

She had heard a step in the gallery
which led from the hall, through the
left wing of the house, to the garden.
The next moment Captain Ryder, putting his hand before his eyes as if dazzled
by the change from the darkness outside
to the lamplight, stumbled past her.

Nanny wanted to put out her arms to
him, to raise the head bent with grief, to
tell him to take comfort, for she would
nurse him back to health and reason.
But a strange reticence had seized her.
In the presence of that coarse, vindictive
woman she could not make one step.
She felt, too, now for the first time, a
chill doubt whether even her love would

avail to break down the barrier which
his malady had raised between herself
and him.

This man, who slunk past her with
head hung down and shuffling steps,
scarcely seemed the same Dan who had
held her in his arms and looked with
wistful, tender, yearning love into her
face only the previous morning. Nanny
felt that she had said good-bye, for the
time at least, to the Dan whose love had
made her happiness ; but to the restless,
unhappy creature before her must be
paid the debt of gratitude she owed for
the sunshine of her early married days.

When he reached the middle of the
hall, he stopped, looked up at the lamp,
and passed his hand through his curly
gray hair as Nanny had often seen him
do. Should she go to him now ? The

poor child was so much afraid of being repulsed in the sight of Mrs. Durrant; if they had been unwatched, she would have flown to his side, encouraged by the familiar action. But now she hesitated. Suddenly he moved forward with quicker steps. Nanny watched him, trembling and heart-sick. He had caught sight of the case of spirits which she had not had time to push quite into the corner she had destined for it.

In a moment Ralph Ryder had seized the case, examined it, turned it up on end, and was trying with his fingers to force the rough planks apart. . He dragged at the wood until he tore the flesh of his hands ; he raised the case and knocked it against the wall, in a furious attempt to loosen the well-driven nails. Finally he dashed it down on the ground,

evidently in the hope that the bottles
would break, and that some of the
precious liquid would run out, to be
scooped up as well as might be. But
it was too well packed; his efforts were
all in vain. He looked around him,
either not seeing or not caring that
Nanny stood, with tightly-clasped hands,
at the bottom of the staircase. Fortunately, Valentine Eley had taken the
precaution to take the hammer away
with him when he fastened up the
case.

But the fact scarcely brought relief to
Nanny. She saw in the glowing gray
eyes an expression of resolution which
she knew in Dan; and she knew that,
mad as he might be, he would not rest
until he had attained his object.

A low cry escaped her lips. Even the

callous Mrs. Durrant was moved, or
interested, or alarmed.

' Ralph, Ralph !' she suddenly called
to him, with a sharpness which com-
manded attention, 'put that case down,
there's a good fellow—put it down, I
say !'

But he only glanced up, paying no
heed.   Then Nanny summoned her
failing courage, ran across the hall to
him, and put her hand upon his arm.
He staggered back, looked at her, and,
with a sudden, not loud, but most
piercing cry, turned and fled out of the
hall into the grounds.

Trembling like a leaf, Nanny followed.   Not knowing her way, she
stumbled blindly along, and, more by
chance than by judgment, she at last
found herself out in the grounds, with

the night-air blowing coldly upon
her.

Where was he going? To The
Grange? She hoped, and yet feared,
that it might be so : hoped, because she
still clung to the belief that love might
do more than medicine; feared, because
in that one moment when her eyes had
met his, she had seen with frightful
clearness what a change in him his
malady had already wrought.

At first, coming from light to darkness, she could see nothing; she dashed
her face against the sharp little leaves of
a yew-tree, and tore her dress in a tangle
of thistle and bramble, before her feet
sank in the long, soft, damp grass of an
overgrown lawn. Then she had to stop,
for she had lost sight of the object of her
pursuit, and she could hear nothing but

the tree-tops rustling in the night-wind, and the faint sound of Mrs. Durrant's discordant laughter in the house behind her. Nanny felt so desolate, so frightened on finding herself thus alone in this wilderness, out of which she knew no way of escape, that her heart failed her, and she burst into childish tears. A full sense of her calamity seemed to fall upon her for the first time ; she was a widow in the first days of marriage, with an awful secret in her heart at which she scarcely dared to look. Her sobs, however, did reach a not unpitying ear. She was still close under the wall of the house. Raising the window of one of the kitchen offices ever so softly and ever so little, the maid-servant who had let Nanny in hissed out, in a loud whisper :

'Don't take on so, ma'am. If you're looking for the Captain, I saw him go by, and I think he's gone off to Pickering's cottage, just inside the grounds, away to the left. Right through the trees and everything you must go until you come to it.'

'Thank you—oh, thank you!' cried Nanny, as she dashed off in the direction indicated by the girl.

Difficult enough it was in the darkness to stumble through the jungle-like growth of grass and thistle, shrub and tree. She shivered, more with fright than cold, as a gust of wind would come and bring down upon her head and shoulders a shower of dried leaves. At last she came upon the cottage, a good-sized one, entirely hidden from the outside world by trees, and by the high wall which enclosed the grounds. A flickering light, which fell from two of the ground-floor windows on the foliage outside, showed Nanny that in all probability the girl had directed her rightly. Since Pickering was away, this illumination was probably the work of Captain Ryder. She stole round the cottage and looked in through the first window which had a light in it. She saw a tiny room, containing a chair-bedstead not in use, and a few simple articles of furniture. There was a lighted candle on the mantelpiece, but no one was in the room. From the adjoining apartment, however, there came a loud noise, like the dragging about of a heavy box. Nanny looked in through the next window.

The second room was a small kitchen,

and in it Nanny saw Captain Ryder,
dragging a box along the floor. With a
key taken from the dresser he unlocked
this box, which proved to be a tool-
chest, took from it a heavy wooden
mallet and a small hatchet, and slammed
the lid down with an exclamation of
triumph. Then, with the rapidity of a
fixed resolution, he kicked away from
him the tool-chest, overthrowing the
lighted candles in his haste, and quitting
the cottage by a door on the other side,
dashed past Nanny on his way back to
the house.

She leaned back against the cottage
wall, for the moment too sick with fear
to move away. She knew the purpose
for which he had got those tools; she
knew that he meant to prise open the
case of spirits. But that was only the

beginning of what she feared. A madman, brooding over his misfortunes,
excited by strong drink, with those tools
in his possession ! What would it mean?
what would it mean?

And a hideous whisper came to answer
her : It would mean again what it had
meant before, when the drink-frenzy had
seized him and urged him to a crime
which he had only been able to wipe out
by a supposititious death. It would mean
again, as it had meant before—murder!

CHAPTER VIII.

As Nanny leaned against the wall of Pickering's cottage, with her heart full of the most terrible fears, listening to the rustle of the dried leaves on the ground as the unhappy maniac made his way through them towards the house, she was startled by a sudden flash of light on to the trees opposite the cottage windows. She looked into the kitchen, whence the light seemed to come, and saw that the place was on fire. Ralph Ryder had overturned the candle without extinguishing it, and the flame had caught an old newspaper which had been lying on the floor, and had spread thence to the nearest leg of the table, round which smoke and flame were now playing.

Nanny found the door and hurried in. Already the atmosphere was thick and stifling. She had passed a pump outside the cottage, and luckily a pail was at hand; so with some difficulty and much exertion she succeeded in putting out the fire, not, however, before she had drenched both the floor and her own clothes with water. This work had for a time chased away even the terrors which had possessed her. It left her so much exhausted from fright, as well as unusual exertion, that she was glad to sit down, still coughing and panting in the smoke, on a chair in the flooded kitchen.

The only discoverable box of matches had been burnt in the conflagration, so that all the light she had came from the candle in the adjoining room. But, from the manner in which it flickered and jumped, Nanny perceived that its end was near, and that she would soon be altogether in darkness.

Just as the candle spluttered and went out, a man's footsteps sounded on the stones outside, and the next moment Nanny heard Pickering's rough voice, crying angrily :

'Hallo! what's up? Who's there?'

'It is I, Pickering—Mrs. Ryder,' Nanny tried to say; but her voice was still hoarse from the smoke, and she only succeeded in uttering a wheezy, husky whisper, at the meaning of which the gardener had evidently to guess.

'My lady! Here! *Is* it my lady?' cried the man in astonishment. But he took it for granted that it was, for he went on: 'Well, and to think of my having gone all the way to-day for to see you, and then to think you was here all the time! And a bad job it is I had to tell you about, too. But what's happened here? It smells o' burning, and—and the place is full of water! Dear me, it's the Captain been up to his tricks again, I suppose.'

'You would have been burned out, Pickering, if I hadn't seen it through the window,' said Nanny, still hoarse and choking. 'What—what was it you had to tell me?'

She felt that it was mean of her to take advantage of the mistake he had made, but this old matter of the identity

of Lady Ellen was so vitally interesting
to her that the hope of finding out something concerning her mysterious rival
proved too strong for Nanny's honesty.

'I went to tell you, my lady, as how
Mrs. Durrant had come back, and that
there was mischief brewing. And as how
she'd got the Captain back to the house
again, with one of his fits threatening,
and as how she drinks more than she
ought, and if the Captain gets hold of
the stuff when he's in one of his
tantrums, even she won't be able to
manage him.'

Nanny uttered an exclamation of
horror. Pickering went on :

'And I was going to make bold to
say to you, my lady, as how, no offence
to you, somebody at The Grange ought
to be told how the land lay. The little

lady there will get such a fright some of these days as'll do her no good.   Now, if so be——'

He stopped, startled.   Nanny had sprung up, with her fears full upon her at this suggestion ; and even in the darkness the old gardener perceived, as he hunted about the room for his matches, that he had made a mistake.

'Bless my soul!' he muttered to himself, 'if I haven't been and made a thundering ass of myself——'

Without another audible word he went on groping about, until presently he produced from a cupboard a candle and matches, struck a light, and came face to face with young Mrs. Ryder.

'I thought so,' said he, shaking his head ; 'but it was an unkind trick to play an old man, ma'am.'

'No,' said Nanny, whose white face confirmed the truth of the words he had uttered concerning her, 'I did tell you who I was, and it was not my fault that I was too hoarse for you to understand me. And I cannot be blamed for using any means to find out what you yourself confess I ought to be told. Now, who is Lady Ellen? And where does she live?'

Pickering shook his head again.

'I've served the family forty years, ma'am,' he said respectfully but firmly, 'and I've taken Lady Ellen's part through thick and thin for thirty of them. And I can't play turncoat now. I wish she'd be open with you; I do indeed, ma'am. But it's not for me to speak when she keeps her mouth shut.'

'Will you tell me just this: when

you went to see her to-day, they told
you she was not at home ?'

' Yes, ma'am.'

' Now, where did they say she had
gone ?'

Pickering hesitated.

' I don't know, ma'am, as I ought to
tell you even that.'

Nanny stepped forward to one side of
the burnt and blackened table, as the old
man stood on the other. Leaning upon
it, she gazed across at him with a look
in her large gray eyes which no man
could have resisted.

' I have no friend in the world to tell
me anything,' she said. ' I am left to
struggle with the most frightful trouble
all alone. Can you deny that? Can
you refuse to tell me just that little
thing ?'

Pickering was not demonstrative. He gave one shy side-glance at her unhappy face, and promptly turned away from her.

'She's gone to Edinburgh,' he said shortly.

' Edinburgh !' echoed Nanny in great excitement.

For was not Meg there, who might be set to play detective ?

'So they said. I can't answer for it that it's true.'

' No, of course not,' agreed Nanny, suddenly moderating her transports in fear lest he should grow too cautious again. 'And do you know to what part of Edinburgh ?'

' No, ma'am.'

' Nor the name of the people to whom she was going ?'

Pickering moved from one foot to another uneasily, still with no more than a side view of his face presented to the lady. But all at once he seemed to make up his mind, and, turning swiftly round to face her, though he judiciously kept his eyes from encountering the plaintive look on her face, and fixed them instead on the dresser behind her, he brought his hand down on the table with a force which cracked and splintered the burnt leg :

' Now look 'e here, ma'am. I'm not going to answer one more question after this, and I don't know as I'm· doing right to answer this one. But I will. And if, like a many of you ladies, you are clever enough to find out more from a nod than plenty men would from a day of talk, why, that's not my fault.

They told me as Lady Ellen had gone
to Edinburgh to see a Miss Anstruther,
but I don't know whether her ladyship
goes by her own name up there.'

Nanny remembered the name of Miss
Anstruther as that of the lady who had
given Meg only too accurate information
about the secret of the Ryders. She
must, then, have returned from her
Australian voyage. Here was a clue at
last by which to discover the mysterious
Lady Ellen. If Meg could find out the
lady who was staying with Miss Anstruther and give a description of her,
Nanny felt that she would be able to
find Lady Ellen out on her return to the
South, under whatever name she chose
to pass. She stood speechless with excitement at the thought.

Pickering glanced at her with pity in

his eyes. He was curious to know how
much she had gleaned of the family
secret, and he was exceedingly anxious,
on the other hand, to have her safely
out of the domain of The White House.

‘ May I make so bold as ask how you
got in, ma’am ?’ he asked at last.

‘ The servant this Mrs. Durrant
brought with her from Teddington let
me in. It was not the girl’s fault,’
Nanny hastened to add, as she saw the
old gardener frown ; ‘ she thought it
was you. She wanted you because—
because he—Captain Ryder—was at the
house, and there was a great case of
spirits about. He came here just now
and opened your tool-chest and——’

‘ The Captain it was who opened it !’
cried Pickering in alarm. ‘ I must be
off to the house, ma’am, begging your

pardon,' he went on, as a rapid inspection
of the chest told him that it had been
rifled. ' He's not to be trusted with
such tools as he's taken when there are
spirits about, and one of his fits coming
on him.'

Nanny trembled at this confirmation
of her fears.

' Oh, Pickering, you don't think——'
she began, and stopped.

' You must let me put you safely outside first, ma'am,' he said, signing to her
respectfully, but peremptorily, to precede
him out of the cottage.

But Nanny lingered one moment, and
shook her heard.

' No,' she whispered hoarsely, ' I am
going up to the house with you. I
must see him again. I don't feel afraid
of him even now. I believe that, if I

can only speak with him alone for a few
moments—not before that woman, but
alone—I could quiet him better than
she, or than you, or anybody.'

Pickering shook his head with appa-
rent surprise at her boldness. She had
left the cottage, and was making her
way, he following, through the wilderness of shrub-growth towards the house.

' No,' he said. ' What could you do,
ma'am ? It takes a lifetime o' knowledge
of mad folks and their ways to do any
good with 'em.'

' Not if you love them, not if you
love them,' she answered earnestly.' ' If
he were just a stranger, I am sure I
should feel dreadfully frightened, and I
should enrage him the more by showing
it. But as it is, knowing all the while
that he is my own husband and that he

loves me, I only feel as I did when he was ill and didn't know me. And if he were ever so violent, I should feel certain he would not hurt me.'

Pickering listened to this speech in great perplexity. For a few moments he followed her silently. A light rain was pattering through the half-bare trees on to their faces, and behind the great square house flimsy little clouds could be seen driving swiftly across the face of the moon. A light was being carried about backwards and forwards, apparently from one room to another, on the first-floor, and a second light could be seen travelling upwards through the staircase window.

' That's Mrs. Durrant's servant going upstairs to bed,' said Pickering, clearly glad to change the subject. ' But the

second light—I don't know what that
is, unless it's Mrs. Durrant and her
brother quarrelling again.'

He quickened his steps, being evidently anxious. He tried as he went to
dissuade the lady from entering the house
again, but, failing in that attempt, he
was silent with an obstinate silence which
Nanny did right in not mistaking for
acquiescence. For, on arriving at the
back-door of the house, and finding it
locked, he said quietly :

'You see, ma'am, we can't either
of us get in to-night, however much
we might want to. We're locked
out.'

'No, we're not,' said Nanny quietly.
'I heard that wicked woman say that he
would make straight for The Grange and
frighten me, so it is certain she will

have left open some way for him to
come by.'

Pickering was shocked.

' Did she say that ?' he said incredu-
lously. ' You must have mistaken her
meaning, ma'am, I'm thinking. It's
not natural for one woman to talk so
of another, barring she's suffered great
wrong.'

' Let us look about,' Nanny went
on, ' and we shall find a way of
getting in.'

She was curious, but no longer so
anxious, as to what was taking place
inside the house. Pickering's presence
had done much to reassure her. For,
on reflection, it seemed pretty certain
that Valentine Eley would have taken
advantage of Captain Ryder's expedition
to the cottage to hide the case of spirits,

and having done so, he would be dis-
creet enough to take himself out of the
way of the maniac's revenge.

Pickering, evidently alarmed by young
Mrs. Ryder's revelations, left her with
an exclamation of dismay to try another
side-door from the garden into the house.
Nanny, thus left for a moment alone,
went up the steps to the raised veranda
which ran from end to end at the back
of the building. She had to tear her
way through a tangle of wistaria, cle-
matis and Virginia creeper, the luxuriant
growth of which, unchecked by any sort
of care, almost blocked one end of the
veranda. Forcing her way through,
Nanny discovered that one of the long
French windows, of which there were
several on this side of the house, was
open, confirming her fears. She slipped

inside, and found that she was in a small room, opening on the other side into the hall, and close to the door of Captain Ryder's apartment.

Overhead she heard sounds of rapid footsteps, and of voices in loud discussion. Only Mrs. Durrant's tones could be distinguished, as they rose from time to time to a pitch at which they almost became screams. It was clear that, as Pickering had surmised, a quarrel was taking place. Mrs. Durrant was apparently continuing with her brother the angry discussion about Captain Ryder the beginning of which Nanny had overheard. But surely they were growing very violent! She listened to the noise of footsteps going hither and thither until it seemed to her that there must be a chase going on. She wished Pickering had come in with her. Running to the window, she called to him; but he was out of hearing, and she got no answer.

In the meantime, the noise above was increasing so greatly as to cause Nanny considerable alarm. It seemed to her that some sort of scuffle must be taking place almost immediately over her head; and she came to the conclusion that Valentine, finding persuasion of no avail against his sister's obstinate intentions of mischief, was constrained to use physical force in order to restrain her. At that moment the noise of some heavy piece of furniture being thrown to the ground startled her greatly, especially as it was accompanied by a sound like a woman's cry.

Nanny rushed out into the hall, and

was making for the staircase, when her
attention was arrested by the figure of a
man standing in the shadow of the
drawing-room door, which was half
open.

'Dan!' she cried at once. And
believing the man to be her husband,
she followed him as he at once softly
disappeared into the room. 'Dan! dear
Dan!' she repeated, as she groped in the
darkness, half afraid of her own venture-
someness, but determined to profit by
this chance of an interview alone with
him. Had not Mrs. Durrant herself
said that the poor fellow, in his frenzy,
would 'go straight to The Grange *after
his wife?*' What, then, had she to fear,
in the face of this proof that, even in
his madness, he thought first of her?
The noise upstairs, moving now away,

as if the scuffle had again given place to
a chase, continued and grew, if anything,
louder than before. Nanny was impressed by the necessity of coming to
terms with her husband before the
quarrel upstairs should end, and one or
both of the disputants break in upon
their privacy. Again, as she pursued
him through the bare and silent rooms,
he eluded her, creeping round by the
walls, so that sometimes she could only
track him by the creak of a board, or by
the sound of his foot brushing against
the strips of damp paper that hung down
over the wainscoting.

It cannot be said that the unhappy
young wife felt no pangs of nervous fear
as she continued to call her husband's
pet name in vain, and to pursue from
end to end of the long suite of rooms

the stealthy figure. Was he, in his
madness, luring her as far as possible out
of the reach of human help, only to turn
upon her in an access of senseless fury,
as he had done upon his own child?
She remembered the mallet he had taken
from the chest: one blow with it might
easily be fatal. The thought was such a
horrible one that poor Nanny stopped
for an instant, with the blood running
cold in her veins. The next moment
she had recovered herself, and was again
pursuing him. If, indeed, his poor mad
brain should prompt him to this, would
not death at his hands be better than
the fate which was now before her, the
life of the living tied to the dead?

In that one moment's pause she had
missed him again, and she presently
found that he had doubled, passing her

in the darkness, and was making for the door by which they had both entered.

He would escape her again.

' Dan, my husband, stay one moment, and listen to me !' she cried again in her tenderest tone.

And, springing forward in her eagerness to detain him, she did indeed touch the man's hand, only, however, to withdraw her own with a cry. For the fingers she had touched were wet, and a subtle, unaccountable instinct told her that it was with blood.

They were both near the door. Nanny ran out into the hall, where there was light. Her instinct had been a right one : there was a horrible stain on her hand.

While she still stared at it in mute

horror, the steps of the man she had
pursued sounded softly behind her.

It was Valentine Eley. His collar
was gone, his coat was torn, and the
hand she had touched was cut and
bleeding. His face was ghastly, and his
voice hoarse as he answered her.

' Not Captain Ryder !' she hissed out.
' Then where is he ?'

' With my sister—upstairs.'

' What ?' cried Nanny, drawing a long
breath of terror. ' My husband —
upstairs—with your sister ! Then he is
killing her !'

And turning towards the staircase,
with a few swift steps she had almost
reached it, when Valentine's hands,
seizing her arm with a firm grasp, from
which the comparatively feeble woman
could not escape, held her back.

'Don't go, don't go!' he cried. 'What is the use? She can manage him if anyone can. It is death for anybody else to go near him.'

'But they have been struggling. I have heard them. It may be life and death for her. I believe it *is*,' quavered Nanny, still striving with all her might to mount the stairs.

'Listen!' cried Valentine; and his white face seemed to grow livid and gray as he spoke. 'Listen! He is like a wild beast to-night. It is her fault, and she must suffer for it. He cannot hurt her much; she is strong, and she can seize moments to calm him. There was spirit brought into the house, as you know. While he was gone just now—I didn't know where to; I thought to The Grange—I hid the case.

But when he came back and did not
find it, he missed it, and was angry.
He ran upstairs into the room where I
was sitting with my sister. And to
pacify him, as she said, she let him taste
the whisky. I told her she was mad,
and she laughed at me. Of course he
became excited; he wanted more; he
would have more; it intoxicated him
at once, made him dangerous—mur-
derous. I tried to seize the decanter,
to take it away. The action enraged
him. He had a mallet in his hands,
brought, I think, to open the case with.
He flew at me, seized me, struck at me;
you can see for yourself what he did to
me before I managed to escape.'

'Yes, but your sister! How could
you leave her? She is not safe with
him!'

Valentine looked troubled.

' She said she was.   She herself helped
me to get out of the room, and locked
the door.'

' But that has enraged him.   I im-
plore you, I entreat you, come upstairs !
Call to Pickering.   He is outside.   We
must break in and save her.'

It was cowardice, personal cowardice,
Nanny felt sure, which induced Valentine to believe, or to affect to believe,
that their interference would make
matters worse.   As a matter of fact,
she was wrong.   Having an enormous
trust in his sister's power both of 'will
and of management, the young man had,
as usual, allowed himself to be a mere
cipher in her hands; and it required all
Nanny's entreaties and menaces to induce
him to let her interfere.   At last most

reluctantly he let her go, and followed her upstairs.

They had scarcely reached the landing, however, when sounds reached their ears which told both him and his companion that they had not come a moment too soon.

Rapid footsteps, heavy breathing, followed by the throwing up of a window-sash, half-stifled cries as of a person gagged and helpless, a savage growl like that of a wild animal, and then, shrill and clear, the woman's cry of: 'Help! help! It's murder!'

The madman and his victim were struggling in a death-grapple. Of this there could be no doubt. The door was locked. Nanny flung herself with all her force upon it, and, dragging Valentine forward, made him do the same.

It shook, it rattled, but it stood the strain.

The frightened woman inside, hearing voices, and hoping that help was at hand, rushed to the door, only to be dragged back and flung on the floor. A hoarse, horrible laugh—a laugh so fiendish that Nanny never forgot it—broke from the madman's lips.

Nanny rushed to the staircase-window, smashed a pane with her bare hand, and shrieked at the top of her voice :

' Pickering ! Pickering !'

A shout answered her.

' Quick ! quick !' she cried, in a voice of agony.

But even as her cry rang out through the air, another and yet more piercing scream came from the locked-up room :

the sound of a heavy blow, another struggle, a feeble cry, and a heavy, sliding fall.

Then came dead silence.

END OF VOL. II.

BILLING AND SONS, PRINTERS, GUILDFORD.
St. & Hy.

www.ingramcontent.com/pod-product-compliance
Lightning Source LLC
Chambersburg PA
CBHW020351030726
47496CB00007B/2106